SPECIAL MESSAGE TO READERS

This book is published under the auspices of

THE ULVERSCROFT FOUNDATION

(registered charity No. 264873 UK)

Established in 1972 to provide funds for research, diagnosis and treatment of eye diseases. Examples of contributions made are: —

A Children's Assessment Unit at Moorfield's Hospital, London.

•

Twin operating theatres at the Western Ophthalmic Hospital, London.

•

A Chair of Ophthalmology at the Royal Australian College of Ophthalmologists.

•

The Ulverscroft Children's Eye Unit at the Great Ormond Street Hospital For Sick Children, London.

You can help further the work of the Foundation by making a donation or leaving a legacy. Every contribution, no matter how small, is received with gratitude. Please write for details to:

THE ULVERSCROFT FOUNDATION,
The Green, Bradgate Road, Anstey,
Leicester LE7 7FU, England.
Telephone: (0116) 236 4325

In Australia write to:
THE ULVERSCROFT FOUNDATION,
c/o The Royal Australian and New Zealand College of Ophthalmologists,
94-98, Chalmers Street, Surry Hills,
N.S.W. 2010, Australia

RETURN OF THE VALKO KID

Marshal Clem Everett is summoned to Austin by Governor Hyram Sloane to track down a gang of outlaws led by Black Bill Bodie. His mission is to recover a document Bodie has stolen. Bodie is the fastest draw alive and only the outlaw Valko Kid has any chance of beating Black Bill. Sloane agrees to pardon Valko if the pair can retrieve the document. Clem Everett and the Valko Kid set off after Bodie to face untold carnage in their quest.

Books by Michael D. George
in the Linford Western Library:

THE VALLEY OF DEATH
THE WAY STATION
DEATH ON THE DIXIE
KID PALOMINO
RIDERS OF THE BAR 10
IRON EYES
THE GUNS OF TRASK
THE SHADOW OF VALKO
GHOST OF THE GUNFIGHTER
THE VALKO KID
THE MYSTERIOUS MESA
CODE OF THE BAR 10
PALOMINO RIDER
THE SPURS OF PALOMINO
THE PINTO RIDER
PALOMINO SHOWDOWN

MICHAEL D. GEORGE

RETURN OF THE VALKO KID

Complete and Unabridged

LINFORD
Leicester

First published in Great Britain in 2004 by
Robert Hale Limited
London

First Linford Edition
published 2005
by arrangement with
Robert Hale Limited
London

British Library CIP Data

George, Michael D.
Return of the Valko kid.—Large print ed.—
Linford western library
1. Western stories
2. Large type books
I. Title
823.9′14 [F]

ISBN 1–84617–091–5

Published by
F. A. Thorpe (Publishing)
Anstey, Leicestershire

Set by Words & Graphics Ltd.
Anstey, Leicestershire
Printed and bound in Great Britain by
T. J. International Ltd., Padstow, Cornwall

This book is printed on acid-free paper

Dedicated with respect
to the memories of
Gene Autry and Alex Gordon,
see you in Sioux City, boys.

1

The Governor's mansion was a marble edifice which stood amongst a half-dozen other similar tributes to Texan prosperity in the very heart of Austin. This was a city which bore little if any resemblance to the rest of what was known as the Wild West. It was part of the necklace of capital cities that had spread from the District of Columbia across the States and territories as America grew ever larger.

Austin was a place where power protected the well-heeled from the gruesome realities which lay just outside their well-guarded domains. It was, like all its cousins, a city that no honest eyes could look upon without feeling slightly guilty. Yet those within its city limits had seldom given those less fortunate than themselves a first thought, let alone a second. They lived whilst the majority of Texans simply tried to exist.

Two totally different worlds inhabited by people who could not be more different. Even the servants here had more than most of the people outside the boundaries of Austin.

Veteran US Marshal Clem Everett had been summoned from Waco by an urgent yet strange telegram from Jacob Francis, the Governor's personal secretary. When he also received a letter containing more than a hundred dollars to cover his expenses, the marshal dismissed his reservations and booked his ticket at the Wells Fargo office.

Everett had no idea why the most powerful man in Texas would want to see him. He knew that Governor Hyram Sloane was not someone who wasted his time having meetings with total strangers. Especially those who came from outside his civilized circle of friends and colleagues.

If anything, Sloane was known for his total disregard for his state's citizens.

He was a man who had a lavish life style that was superior to that of many of his Eastern counterparts in Washington DC. Marshal Everett would normally have ignored the telegraph message, had it not come from the Governor's office.

The lavish expenses only added to the puzzle.

What did Sloane want with a mere US marshal? What could Clem Everett provide for this powerful politician that no one in Austin seemed capable of?

Everett knew that few men in his profession were even acknowledged by, let alone summoned to the state capitol. It troubled the veteran lawman.

Yet for all his concern, the marshal was curious.

Curiosity had lured the lawman like a candle draws moths to its deadly flame. With the hard cash in his wallet, Everett had put on his Sunday best, strapped his gunbelt around his hips and boarded the stagecoach willingly.

The journey had been a hard but

educational one. The marshal had been surprised by the obvious affluence which greeted his eyes the closer he got to the centre of Austin. He could not have imagined that such a place existed, not even in his wildest dreams, if he had not witnessed it with his own eyes from the stagecoach windows. It made him feel like a beggar being taken into a valley full of palaces.

The tall lawman had paced around the impressive reception hall, waiting to be ushered into the inner sanctum of the Governor's private chambers for nearly an hour. The cold marble walls and floors seemed to have the ability somehow to chill the hot Texan air down to a tolerable temperature.

Yet beads of sweat still managed to force themselves below the brim of his large Stetson from the pores on his temples.

Everett glanced up at the beautiful wall clock for the umpteenth time and noted that he had now been here for more than an hour. Yet he knew that he could not complain. He had arrived late the previous evening and found that a luxurious room in Austin's best hotel had been reserved for him. No expense had been spared for the stranger from Waco.

He had been awoken at eight and then escorted across Austin to the government buildings. Everett had started to get nervous as he wondered whether he was here under false pretences. Had Sloane mistaken him for some other Clem Everett?

Was he actually in trouble? He shook his head. How could he be? The Governor of Texas would not splash out money to someone who was in his bad books.

Another thought filled his mind.

What if he had been brought here for some sinister purpose?

He knew that there were no lower creatures on the face of the earth than those who dwelled in the cesspit of politics. The palms of his hands rested on the grips of his guns and he brooded. Did Sloane think he was a killer for hire? A man who was little better than the outlaws he had spent a lifetime hunting down?

He used the tails of his bandanna to mop the sweat from his hardened features, then he noticed the eyes of the other men waiting in the large hall.

Since his arrival he had felt like a fish out of water. His attire was totally different from that of every other man in the capital city. He wore a Stetson and what passed for fashionable clothing in Waco, yet here top hats adorned almost every head and the clothes were of a style he had never seen before.

Every passing minute made the lawman more anxious.

Then, just as he had placed a cigar between his teeth, the twelve-foot-high double-doors opened to reveal the thin pale figure of Jacob Francis.

'Come this way, Marshal. The Governor will see you now.'

Everett heard the almost feminine voice echo all around him off the shining walls. He removed the cigar and walked towards the man.

Francis led the way across the spacious outer office to another set of doors which were of equal height and splendour to the ones which graced the hall.

The private secretary gave the doors a gentle tap with his pink knuckles, then opened them. He himself did not enter but gestured with his right arm for Everett to do so.

The marshal removed his Stetson and walked towards the mahogany desk. He heard the doors being closed behind him as he reached the seated figure.

'You sent for me, Governor?'

Sloane was a man who looked even paler than Jacob Francis. His bald head and thin features appeared never to have been out in the Texas sun at any time during the day. He looked like a man who had lived his entire life indoors.

'You are Clem Everett of Waco?'

'Yep.' Everett nodded as he held his hat before him by the brim, the way a bride might grip nervously on to her bouquet. 'I hope I'm the man that you wanted to see. I've had me a few doubts about that.'

'You are the man I wanted to see, Marshal,' Governor Sloane confirmed.

Clem Everett felt as if a weight had been lifted off his broad shoulders when he heard those words.

'I'm mighty relieved about that, sir.'

Sloane pointed across the large desk to the seat opposite his own. 'Sit down. We have to talk.'

The tall lawman did as he was instructed. He placed his hat on his knee and stared across the desk at the Governor.

'I'm still confused, sir. How come ya want to talk with me anyway? I'm just an old-fashioned law officer.'

Hyram Sloane folded his arms.

'I have a job for you.'

Everett felt his left eyebrow rise.

'What kinda job, sir? I'm just a

lawman who chases outlaws for a living. I reckon I'd not fit in around here.'

Sloane leaned forward and placed both his hands on his ink blotter. His small eyes were riveted to the lawman.

'You misunderstand, Marshal. The job I have for you has nothing to do with your working in Austin. Far from it. I require your expertise in the hunting down and elimination of ruthless outlaws.'

Clem Everett was silent for a few moments as he tried to absorb the words that came from the man's mouth. He rubbed his firm jaw.

'You need some outlaws caught, killed or hung?'

The expression on the face of the Governor changed. He smiled.

'Exactly.'

Everett felt uneasy.

'I still don't quite understand. How come ya want me to hunt down some outlaws and hang them? Surely you've got enough lawmen in this city to do that for you?'

The Governor cleared his throat and rose to his feet. His eyes never left the seated marshal.

'You are correct. We have a lot of peace officers in Austin, Marshal. But they are not men like yourself. They are mere shadows of real lawmen.'

'Shadows?'

Sloane walked to a table near one of the three windows in the office. He removed the glass stopper from one of the crystal decanters and then lifted it up and poured two large measures into round, stemmed glasses.

'You do drink whiskey, I take it?'

'Yep. I can drink as much as you care to give me, sir.'

The Governor nodded and cupped the glasses in his hands. He walked to Everett and gave one to the marshal, then returned to his own padded leather chair.

'Yes, Marshal. Shadows. These men are not cut from the same cloth as yourself. These are mere shadows of your type. They wave sticks at drunken wretches on Saturday nights. Give them a gun and they'd more than likely shoot themselves. No, Marshal, they are not lawmen like you. That is why I've enlisted you for this very delicate mission. You are very well-known to myself. I feel that you will accomplish this mission admirably.'

'With due respect, I ain't said that I'm agreeable yet, sir,' Clem Everett said. He lifted his glass to his lips and sipped at its contents.

Sloane smiled even more widely.

'You are exactly as I've been led to believe you are. You are no fool and this job requires a cool, clear head on the shoulders of an experienced law enforcer.'

'Reckon?' Everett finished his whiskey and placed the glass on the desk. 'I need more information than you've given me before I'll agree to do anything. I don't cotton to flattery, sir.'

'I'm sorry.' The bald man shrugged. 'You are right. I have flattered you and not seen fit to explain what it is that I require you to do. I apologize.'

Everett nodded.

'Apology accepted, sir.'

Sloane drank his own whiskey, then stared hard into the US marshal's tanned face.

'Have you ever heard of a notorious outlaw called Black Bill Bodie?'

Clem Everett sat forward in his chair.

'I sure have.'

'Good.'

'What's Black Bill done that makes him so darn interesting to the most powerful *hombre* in Texas?' Everett could not conceal his curiosity.

Governor Sloane accepted the flattering remarks.

'He has stolen something of immense delicacy.'

'What has he stolen?'

Sloane pointed to the decanter.

'Bring the whiskey over here, Marshal. We are both in need of further refreshment.'

Everett strode across the room, plucked the decanter off the silver tray and returned to the desk. He filled both of their glasses.

'Explain, Governor.'

'He has stolen something very valuable from me. From Texas actually.' The Governor picked up his recharged glass and sipped at its contents.

'Gold or money?'

'Neither.'

'Jewels?'

The Governor shook his head.

'No, Marshal. Something far more important than mere gems.'

The lawman rubbed his chin thoughtfully. He had no idea what could be more valuable than gold or jewels.

'Now I *am* mixed up, sir.'

'Documents!' Sloane elucidated.

The marshal was confused. He sat down on his chair again and nursed his glass in the palms of his weathered hands.

'Documents?' Everett repeated.

'Correct.'

'You want me to hunt Black Bill

down and hang him for stealing papers?' Everett asked.

'Yes.'

Everett finished his second whiskey and stared into the empty glass thoughtfully.

'This must be a mighty important set of papers if you want the thief hung.'

'I cannot tell you how valuable they are,' Sloane agreed. 'I can only tell you that if this document falls into the wrong hands, it could mean disaster for Texas.'

'That's darn important,' Everett gasped.

'Black Bill Bodie is wanted dead or alive as I recall.' The Governor smiled. 'So I think that he's long overdue to have his neck stretched.'

The lawman shrugged.

'I'm not going to argue about that, sir.'

'He and his entire gang must be prevented from disclosing the information in the documents.' The smile disappeared from Sloane's face.

Everett placed his glass down again. He pulled a cigar from his pocket and placed it between his teeth. He found a match and ignited it with his thumbnail. He cupped the flame and sucked in the smoke. As it drifted from between his teeth he looked hard at the bald man.

'Black Bill is no ordinary outlaw, sir. It's said that he's the fastest gun alive.'

'I have heard this rumour.'

'It ain't no rumour. It's the truth. I ain't good enough to go up against him. It would be suicidal.'

Sloane swallowed the remainder of his whiskey.

'You sound almost afraid.'

'I'm afraid all right, sir,' the lawman admitted. 'If I'm to go up against Black Bill Bodie, I'll need the assistance of a top gun. Someone who has got a chance of matching his speed on the draw.'

'Then enlist the help of a top gun, Marshal. I will cover all of your expenses.'

Clem Everett patted his fingers together thoughtfully before speaking again.

'There's only one man I know who's fast enough to have a chance of getting the better of Black Bill, Governor.'

The governor eased himself forward.

'Who, Marshal?'

Clem Everett stared down at the floor, then looked up into the curious eyes of Hyram Sloane.

'The Valko Kid!'

2

There was a long silence as Hyram Sloane poured each of them more measures from his decanter. The governor had heard the outlaw's name before. He had also read the horrific accounts of the atrocities that had been attributed to the young outlaw. Accounts which made gruesome reading, even for someone who had a vast experience of such literature.

'The Valko Kid? He's a ruthless killer, is he not? Are you insane, man?'

Marshal Clem Everett removed the cigar from his mouth and blew a line of smoke at the marble floor. Then he locked his eyes into those of the man across the desk.

'Nope, Governor. I ain't loco. He ain't a killer like the posters say.'

'How can you make such a statement? I have seen his wanted poster and read a file full of sordid details of his exploits, Marshal Everett,' said Sloane. 'It says that he's a merciless killer of men, women and even children. A rapist and thief. A loathsome character by all accounts. The Valko Kid is even worse than Black Bill Bodie.'

'With respect, sir, the accounts are wrong,' Clem Everett insisted firmly. 'I chased him for over a year. When we eventually met he saved my life.'

Sloane raised his eyebrows in surprise.

'I do not understand. He saved your life, you say?'

'Yep. I have seen with my own eyes the impostor who claims to be the Valko Kid. This animal tried to kill me after dispatching most of my posse and crippling a young female sheriff. The varmint got the drop on me and had me in his sights when Valko shot the gun out of his hand. It was the real Valko who saved my life and got himself badly wounded in the process, sir. I have never met a more civilized man than Valko.'

The governor traced a finger down his cut-crystal decanter. He then lifted his glass to his lips and swallowed half its contents.

'And yet he is still wanted dead or alive?'

'Yep.' Everett sighed. 'I tried to put a good word in for him but nobody will listen. The man who stole Valko's identity keeps adding to his list of crimes. Until someone kills that *hombre*, the Valko Kid will never be a free man.'

'Where is the real Valko Kid, Marshal Everett?' Sloane studied the weathered features of the man before him. 'I take it that you know his whereabouts?'

Everett smiled and touched his temple. He picked up his own glass and sipped at the whiskey.

'I know his exact whereabouts, sir. I could get to him in about three days.'

Governor Sloane suddenly realized that Everett was the man he had been praying for. A man of conviction and sound moral judgement. A man unlike anyone else he had ever encountered in the glittering city of Austin.

'You know where he is and you have kept that secret to yourself?'

Everett nodded. 'Yep. Although he don't know that I have been keeping tabs on him. For two years Valko has been living a peaceful life and keeping his nose clean. Nobody in the small town where he's been living has a clue who he is. It took him almost a year to recover from the injuries inflicted upon him by the impostor. He had tried to track the varmint down, but was injured far too badly, Governor.'

'I admire your honesty, Marshal.' Sloane inhaled deeply and swilled the remainder of his whiskey around in his glass before he finished it. 'You seem to know more about this Valko Kid than anyone else.'

'I do, sir,' Everett agreed.

'You say he was injured. Can he still use his guns? Is he still as fast as you claim he once was?'

'I'd not lie to the most powerful man in Texas, sir.' The lawman shrugged. 'I don't know how fast he is now. All I can tell you is that if he's retained half of his speed with them Colts, he'll be more than a match for Bodie.'

The Governor was impressed.

'He was that fast?'

'I never saw anyone faster, sir.'

Sloane was intrigued. 'If you can persuade the Valko Kid to assist you in this delicate matter, I will give him a complete pardon. I shall ensure that he is publicly exonerated for the crimes of which he has been falsely accused.'

Marshal Clem Everett rose to his feet and inhaled on his cigar. He placed his still half-full glass down on top of the ink blotter and held out his hand to the politician. It was shaken firmly.

'I think that might just sway him, Governor.'

'I hope that you are correct, Marshal. We do not have much time. Those documents must be back in my hands by noon on the twentieth.'

Everett placed his Stetson on his head and pulled its brim down until it covered half his brow.

'And today is the ninth. Eleven days to find Black Bill and get that document back here. Could be a mighty tight schedule, sir.' Hyram Sloane nodded in agreement and watched the tall lawman walk out of his office.

3

It had all started three weeks earlier as the eight horsemen rode through the Texan heat haze and stopped their lathered-up mounts just above the isolated town of Sand Rock. Seven of the riders dismounted and drank the last of their canteens' water whilst their leader, still atop his pinto stallion, silently checked his arsenal of weaponry.

None of the other men had two Winchesters in leather scabbards strapped to their saddles. Nor a pair of ammunition belts crossed over their chests the way he did. The handle of a long razor-sharp Bowie knife protruded from his right boot whilst a pair of matched Remington .44s were holstered to each hip. This was no ordinary rider, but the leader of one of the West's most notorious gangs.

The rider was known as Black Bill Bodie. It was said that he was the fastest gun alive.

Black Bill Bodie was a deadly killer who had carved a reputation for himself in the wilds of the Lone Star State which few if any other outlaws would ever match. Bodie had managed to outlive most of his contemporaries because he was good at what he did.

Yet unlike most men of his profession, he could actually use his variety of guns and rifles. He had been a buffalo-hunter when there had still been buffalo herds roaming the plains. He had learned to kill with ruthless accuracy. It had not taken much for him to aim those weapons in the direction of other men.

In the twenty years that he had ridden on the wrong side of the law, Black Bill had seen his gang constantly change. He had lost count of exactly how many of his followers had been killed in the numerous bank and stagecoach robberies that he had planned and executed. Yet there was not one ounce of remorse for any of them.

The men who rode with Bodie were expendable and knew it. They ignored that fact for a share of the proceeds they knew the deadly outlaw could get them. For Bodie was no mere expert killer, but a man who planned everything in minute detail. It was said that he had spies in high places and used their knowledge to get the drop on the most profitable robberies.

Whatever the truth of the matter was, Black Bill Bodie had led a charmed life. Whilst other gang-leaders had come and gone, he still rode at the head of his own small army unscathed.

It mattered little to him how many of his men got killed along the way when jobs went wrong. They were worthless in his eyes. Black Bill knew that he could always find men of that sort to replace the ones he lost along the way. Men who had little brain and even less courage were ideal recruits to his ever-changing miniature army.

Bodie knew that it was only his mastery of firearms which had allowed him to survive into his fifties. Few other outlaws got close to that age.

He ruled by fear.

Few other outlaws could actually draw their guns from their holsters in a fraction of a heartbeat. He could and they knew it.

It would take someone as skilled as himself to end his profitable career. So far he had not encountered that man.

Sand Rock was a remote town in a desolate place. It had survived on the very edge of a blisteringly hot prairie for three decades because a natural spring defied nature and never ceased sending crystal-clear water up from the bowels of the earth into a small water-hole. The entire town had grown around the water-hole in the shade of the high sand-coloured ridges which fringed the prairie.

That single feature had made Sand Rock a valuable asset to its small community. It had become a place where Wells Fargo knew they could rely upon watering their horses, giving their passengers a break from the constant rocking of the stagecoach journey.

The small town had prospered due to the weekly visits of the two stages that passed through it. The southbound and the northbound coaches had given jobs to all the inhabitants of Sand Rock. Fresh horses to be harnessed into the stagecoach traces were always available. A few stores knew that they could get top prices for their beer, liquor and soda pop from the thirsty passengers, who had time to kill as the teams of horses were changed.

But apart from that Sand Rock had nothing except people who defied the arid land around their tiny oasis.

There was no law and no telegraph office. There had never been any need for such things in Sand Rock. There had never been any trouble in the isolated town. All they had of value was the bountiful supply of fresh spring water.

Yet something had brought the eight riders here to this remote town, and it had nothing to do with water.

Black Bill Bodie was not a man to do anything without having first planned it down to the very last detail. He sat in his saddle watching his men trying to get the stiffness out of their legs as he unscrewed the stopper on his canteen. He finished the water and then hung the empty canteen back on his saddle horn.

The inhabitants of Sand Rock had no idea what was about to happen to their settlement. But it would not be long before they found out.

Bodie reached back to one of the satchels of his saddlebags and pulled out a small greased-paper parcel. He opened it carefully. He picked out the best-looking strip of the beef jerky, bit off a chunk and chewed thoughtfully.

There was a grim determination in his cold calculating eyes as he checked his golden half-hunter watch. It was nearly 11.30 and the merciless sun had yet to reach its zenith. It would get a lot hotter before this day was over, he thought. Bodie waved his hands at the men and growled.

'Get back on ya horses, boys. We got us some business down there.'

The seven outlaws obeyed without question. They grabbed their reins and mounted their exhausted horses. Black Bill watched silently.

'Now I reckon it's time I gave ya all some orders.' Bodie spat the tasteless dried meat from his mouth and threw away the parcel over his shoulder. 'Listen up!'

The outlaws all stared at him with expressions that reminded the deadly gunman of school-children waiting for a teacher to speak.

'This is a big job and no mistake, boys. We have to take control of that little town and then wait a few hours for the southbound stagecoach.' Bodie told them. 'It's due to arrive in Sand Rock at three this afternoon but it could be early, or then again, it might be late. All we know for sure is that it'll arrive. When it does, it's ours.'

One of his men named Frank Grange eased his horse closer and pushed the brim of his hat back off his weathered face. He was a buck-toothed man who drawled more than most.

'We taking the strongbox, Bill? Is that why we come here?'

'Yep.' Bodie answered. 'The strong-box. That's what we're after, Frank.'

'It got gold in it?' Grange continued.

'A bit.'

'You joshing us, Bill? Only a bit?'

Black Bill turned his head and looked straight at the rider beside him. He knew that the outlaw was stupid, yet he was the only truly loyal member of his gang. He smiled and patted the back of the man's worn vest.

'The strongbox has got quite a bit of gold in it, Frank. Enough for us to take us a short vacation down south of the border.'

The man smiled and nodded happily.

'What we gotta do when we gets down there?' asked another of the outlaws, named Jett Clooney.

'We simply kill anyone who looks like he's dumb enough to try and kill us, Jett,' Bodie replied. 'The main thing is that we take over the town until the stage arrives. We do whatever it takes to keep them townsfolk in check.'

'How many folks are down there, Bill?' asked a one-eyed outlaw called Sam Baker.

Black Bill Bodie rubbed his mouth along the back of his sleeve and glanced hard at the man's face.

'Less than forty souls, Sam. A lot less after we're through, I guess.'

The horsemen all laughed. It was a chilling sound that had nothing to do with humour. A sound that Bodie had heard many times over his long career. It always happened just before the men who followed him tasted a fresh kill. It was arousal of the most basic of instincts.

'Seems like we rode an awful long

way just to steal a little gold, boss,' Grange said.

'We could have hit at least three fat banks between El Paso and here, Black Bill,' Baker gruffed. 'Don't make no sense us riding all this damn way just to rob a stagecoach.'

Black Bill sat upright in his saddle. He gathered his reins into his gloved hands and smiled.

'There's something else in that strongbox, boys. Something that I'm told is worth a pretty penny. A document. I figure some darn important dudes will want to buy it back from me once I get my hands on it.'

'How ya know this, Bill?' Clooney asked, rubbing his shirt front.

Black Bill forced a half-smile.

'I got me some powerful friends in Austin, Jett. They tells me things and I pays them good for doing so.'

'So this document is worth more than the gold?'

'Yep. There ain't no saying how much that document is actually worth.'

'Bill's smart, right enough.' Grange chuckled.

The riders moved their mounts around the outlaw. There were no more questions. They knew that even if they asked him more he would simply refuse to answer. For Black Bill Bodie was not a man to share anything valuable with his hired help. They rode and did his bidding.

The eight riders lifted themselves from their saddles and stood in their stirrups as their mounts descended the steep sand-coloured ridge towards the quiet town far below them.

Soon Sand Rock would lose its innocence for ever.

* * *

At first none of the inhabitants of Sand Rock noticed the eight riders coming towards them down the steep ridge. Men, women and even children went about their daily rituals knowing that the southbound stage would arrive later that day, bringing with it money that allowed them to trade with the outside world.

There was no reason why any of them would suspect that this day would be any different from those that had gone before it. No hint of any trouble until the sound of horses' hoofs drifted among the wooden buildings.

No one knew who it was amongst their number who first looked up and spotted the eight heavily armed horsemen approaching. At first the riders were well hidden by the heat haze and clouds of dust which drifted constantly off the arid prairie. Then they became visible to the curious eyes.

Even the town's children knew that these were no normal drifters who had suddenly appeared within their midst. The array of weaponry which gleamed in the morning sun was positive proof of that.

Black Bill Bodie kept jabbing his sharp spurs into the sides of his powerful pinto stallion as he led his seven followers closer and closer to the small gathering of onlookers.

When there were more than a dozen people standing across the small dirt road, Bodie hauled his reins back and stopped his mount.

Dust drifted over the people, who could do nothing but stare up at the hardened faces of the outlaws as they all copied their leader and reined in.

'What you want here?' the oldest of the Sand Rock men asked defiantly. 'This ain't no place for men of your kind. We ain't got nothing but water here. You can have your fill of that but then you have to ride on.'

Bodie did not say a word. He stood in his stirrups and looked either side at his hired guns. Then he returned his attention to the old man, who edged closer.

'You understand?' the old man added.

'I ain't no Mex, old-timer. I understand.' Black Bill said in a tone which concealed his anger. 'I just don't think you should get yourself so worked up. A man your age has to be careful.'

The man pulled away from the hands of his friends and kin and moved even closer to the nose of Bodie's horse. He had both fists clenched as he spoke again.

'We ain't dumb, mister. We can see them guns and all. We know your sort. You ain't welcome here. Now get going.'

Black Bill smiled.

'Nothing worse than a noisy old rooster, is there, boys?'

The riders began to laugh.

'You vermin!' the old man ranted, waving his fist. 'Without them guns, you'd be nothing. Think I'm scared of your type? Well I ain't! We don't want outlaws in Sand Rock. There was a time when I could have taken all of you on.'

The other townsfolk behind the old man moved closer and started to chant at the eight riders.

Suddenly, Black Bill Bodie hauled both his guns from their holsters and fired. His accuracy had lost none of its lethal fury. As the gunsmoke drifted away, the line of horsemen stared down at the bodies spread out across the blood-splattered sand. The sound of women and children screaming out in horror came from the shadows within the buildings.

'Find the rest of them, boys,' Bodie growled. He emptied his spent shells from his guns and started to reload the chambers. 'I want them all dead. Every single one of them. They're making too much noise. Even a deaf stagecoach driver could hear that. Kill them!'

The seven riders spurred their horses and homed in on the wooden buildings. They all had their guns cocked and ready for action.

After seeing the merciless venom that Black Bill Bodie could still dish out, none of his men would ever disobey him again.

Even before Bodie had holstered his guns, the shooting was echoing all around Sand Rock.

Yet the deadly outlaw did not give the massacre a second thought. All he could think about was the stagecoach and its precious cargo. A cargo that he knew would be his in a matter of only a few hours. He pulled his golden half-hunter from his vest pocket and stared at its face.

It was exactly noon.

4

The dust-caked Wells Fargo stagecoach had wound its way south across fifty miles of desolate prairie since its last stop at the distant Indian Wells way station. The quartet of passengers had wondered whether their fare of a hundred dollars in golden eagles had been worth the bone-breaking torture which the bumpy trail had forced them to endure.

Yet none of them had ever mastered the art of riding a horse and that was their only other option if they were to reach the distant Austin.

There were no railtracks through this barren wilderness, for few Eastern companies dared spend their stockholders' money on such a risky venture. The Texas terrain varied so widely that there seemed no way of costing such a daring scheme with any accuracy.

The stagecoach still ruled this land, although it was only a matter of time before its dominance was whittled away by the inevitable coming of the iron horse. Until then, those who wished to travel south did so like the four passengers within the rocking interior of the four-wheeled Wells Fargo vehicle.

Because of the vast distances which the stagecoaches had to cover each day, boredom ate its way into the very souls of the men who guarded the driver with their trusty double-barrelled shotguns. The driver himself never had time to get bored as he held the reins to his six powerful horses in his firm grip, and guided them across the well-used trail. Yet the men who had to sit beside the hard-working drivers had little to do except constantly look out for trouble.

The flat prairie gave outlaws little opportunity to attack the fast-moving stagecoaches and there had been few Indians in this part of Texas for nearly a decade.

Today the shotgun guard had stared into the blinding sunlight for so many hours that he had begun to see mirages in the sickening heat haze which surrounded their coach.

His greatest challenge was to try and not doze off and fall from his precarious perch as the rocking vehicle headed towards the golden ridges before them.

Hour after hour the driver had thrashed his heavy reins down on to the backs of the six-horse team in an effort to keep to his tight schedule.

The route had been travelled so many times in each direction by the weekly stagecoaches that deep grooves had been cut into the sand by the metal wheel-rims. The sagebrush had been trampled beneath the shod hoofs.

An almost barren stretch of sand lay like a scar across the once grassy prairie.

None of the six people who rode the southbound stagecoach that fateful day had an inkling of what lay ahead of them in the remote settlement of Sand Rock.

To each and every one of them, this was just another blisteringly hot day like so many others that they had endured on their journey. Another day to eat the dust which continued to float in through the open windows of their speeding vehicle. A day when their thirst became the only thing that they could think about. A thirst which might be quenched when they reached the crystal-clear waters for which Sand Rock had become famous.

The only thing that altered on the prairie was the position of the sun as it moved across the cloudless blue sky above them.

A couple of miles outside the narrow canyon that led to the small oasis, the driver pulled back on the heavy reins and stopped his coach. Plumes of dry choking dust rolled over the vehicle as the driver pulled his brake-pole back until it locked.

George Jones had worked for Wells

Fargo for a quarter of his long life and was regarded as their best long-haul driver. His ancient appearance belied the muscular body he still retained beneath his baggy clothing. He reached beneath his seat and found the battered brass bugle that lay beside the strong-box.

Jones lifted it up, rubbed his dust-caked mouth along the back of his sleeve and spat. He tried to moisten his lips but there was no spittle.

'Why don't ya just head on in, George?' asked the shotgun guard. 'This blowing the bugle trash is dumb. All it does is scare the eagles and buzzards off them crags.'

The driver sighed heavily.

'Rules is rules, Jack. I blow the bugle and if everything's OK, they blow their bugle back at me. Then I take the stagecoach in.'

'But why?' Jack Tanner was eighteen years younger than his companion and had only been with the company for six months. He was the sort who drifted from one job to another and never quite mastered any of them. 'Why blow that damn thing every time we come to a way station? There ain't no bosses out here to hear ya do it.'

'It's just in case there's trouble ahead, Jack,' Jones insisted. 'I don't make the rules. I just follow 'em.'

'Nothin' ever happens out here, though.' Tanner sighed.

'There was a time when this whole prairie was crawling with Indians, Jack. I've seen me reach this spot with more than twenty arrows stuck in my stage. Then there was the outlaws. A few years ago before they headed north to rob the trains, they used to haunt this prairie like ghosts. I stick to the rules.'

The shotgun guard pulled a half-bottle of whiskey from his coat pocket and winked.

'Wet ya whistle, George?'

The driver smiled. He accepted the bottle and pulled its cork. He swallowed a mouthful of the whiskey, then smiled again as he felt it burning the dust from his throat.

'That's good liquor, boy. Now I could blow a cavalry charge.' Jones lifted his bugle and blew out the two notes he had been taught.

A few seconds passed; then they heard a bugle being blown in the dusty canyon.

'Sounds a bit flat today, George,' said the shotgun guard. He accepted his bottle back and took a swig from the neck himself.

The driver nodded and dropped the brass instrument down beside the strongbox again.

'Yeah, it sure does, Jack. Maybe old Charlie let one of the kids blow it this time.'

'Ya might be right,' Tanner agreed. 'Charlie's got less wind than you.'

There had been no doubts in either man's mind as George Jones released the brake-pole and whipped the reins across the backs of his six-horse team.

The stagecoach rolled down the

slight incline and into the dusty canyon on its fateful journey toward Sand Rock. The sound of the snorting horses echoed off the rocks as the driver guided his team through the almost blinding dust into the heart of the canyon. The scent of fresh water had filled the nostrils of the eager animals, and Jones used every muscle in his body to hold them in check.

The guard's sand-filled eyes focused on the blood-soaked sand ahead of the lead horses. When he realized what the red stains on the white sand were, he quickly reached down for his double-barrelled shotgun.

'What's wrong, Jack?' Jones asked. He pulled back on his reins. 'You look like ya seen one of them ghosts we was talking about.'

'No ghosts, George!' the guard managed to say before his chest exploded into a mess of crimson gore. The sheer impact of the outlaws' bullets sent him flying off the high driver's seat and crashing into the sun-baked ground. The driver wiped his partner's blood from his face and went to whip his team. Then he saw the eight men moving out of the buildings to either side of his stagecoach.

Each of the guns had only one target.

'Don't even think about it, old-timer!' Black Bill Bodie yelled out as he aimed his own smoking guns straight at the confused and terrified Jones. 'You ain't going no place until I say so.'

There was no way that the driver was going to argue with the fearsome outlaw leader.

George Jones dropped his reins and closed his eyes.

They were still shut tight when he heard the doors of his stagecoach being opened and the four passengers viciously dragged from its interior.

With every one of the four shots, the driver shook.

Sweat rolled down from Jones's white hair when he felt the coach rocking and heard outlaws climbing up to his high perch. Their eager hands dragged the strongbox out from beneath his seat.

'Got it, Bill,' Jett Clooney yelled out before he dropped the heavy box down to the ground. 'Ya want me to kill this old fool now?'

'Easy, Jett.' Black Bill Bodie laughed, cocked one of his guns and aimed it at the padlock on the metal box at his feet. He fired, sending a hundred fragments of brass flying in all directions. 'You don't kill nobody until I say so.'

The driver felt the gun pushing into his ribs. He started to pray and opened his eyes.

'Please don't shoot me, son. I ain't nothing but a darn stagecoach driver.'

Clooney did not hear one word. All he could do was stare down at the strongbox, the way that a hungry man looks at food.

Black Bill kicked the lid of the box open and then scooped the thick envelope out from its dark centre. He broke the red seal and checked its contents.

'This is what I want, boys,' Bodie

said. He pushed the valuable document inside his shirt. 'C'mon. Help yourselves to this money. I reckon ya all earned it. I don't even want a share of that gold.'

Jett Clooney dragged the old man aside, jumped down from beside the driver and, with his six companions, began clawing at the three small bags of gold coins.

Bodie walked closer to the stagecoach and looked up into the eyes of the terrified driver. He smiled again. The driver did nothing except shake. It was like looking into the eyes of one's executioner.

'You scared, old man?'

'Yep. I'm real scared, sir.'

Black Bill Bodie holstered one of his guns, then pulled out a folded sheet of paper from his pants' pocket. He stared at it for a few seconds, then returned his attention to the driver above him.

'This is a very important letter. You will take it to the Governor.'

The driver stretched out his arm and

reluctantly accepted the paper. He pushed it carefully into his deep coat-pocket.

'The Governor?'

'Yep. The man himself.' Black Bill nodded. 'You will tell him exactly what happened here and that Black Bill Bodie spared you only because I needed you to deliver that letter.'

The driver swallowed hard. 'You want me tell him your name, sir?'

'Damn right, old-timer. I want the man to know exactly who he's dealing with.'

The driver cautiously picked up his reins again and trembled as he looked down at the fearsome sight of the deadly outlaw leader.

'He'll set the army on ya tail, sir.'

Black Bill shook his head in disagreement.

'I don't think he'll do that. If he does, it'll cost him dearly. You see, I've got something of his that he don't want nobody else seeing.'

Frank Grange was holding two

hand-fulls of golden coins as he moved beside his leader.

'Ain't ya killing him?'

'Nope.'

'Why the heck not, Bill?' Jett Clooney asked from beside the strongbox.

Black Bill glanced at the crouching figure, then kicked the outlaw hard in the chest. The force of the kick sent Clooney and his share of the money crashing into the dust.

''Coz I'm the boss, that's why.'

The driver cleared his throat.

'C . . . can I go now, sir?'

'Yep! But if I find out that you ain't been to the Governor, I'll come lookin' for you. And when I find you, I'll kill you slowly.' Black Bill's grin widened as he raised his gun above his head. He squeezed its trigger and fired.

The driver clung to his reins as his startled team galloped out of Sand Rock and away over the prairie. He would not allow his horses to stop until he felt sure that he was out of the range of the outlaws' weaponry.

Fuelled by fear, the frightened driver continued on and on without water or food until his half-dead team took him to Austin, where he delivered Bodie's note into the hands of Governor Hyram Sloane.

5

Waco was bathed in the golden glow of a hundred streetlamps as the six-horse team was steered through its winding streets towards the stage depot. Even though it was nearly midnight the town was still alive with activity. Music mixed with rowdy voices and cascaded from the countless saloons and dance-halls which had helped Waco earn its reputation. The stagecoach's solitary passenger watched silently from one of its windows until the vehicle came at last to a halt.

The US marshal had spent nearly three days and nights pondering Governor Sloane's words. He had tried vainly to imagine what was in the documents that Black Bill Bodie had intercepted at Sand Rock.

It was impossible.

All he knew for sure was that it had

cost the lives of every living soul in the remote town. Only the driver of the stagecoach had been allowed to live so that he could deliver the grim message from the notorious outlaw into Sloane's hands.

Sloane had told the marshal that if the information contained in the secret papers ever became public, Texas itself might be destroyed. Everett could not imagine how such a thing were possible and yet he knew that Sloane was serious.

Deadly serious.

Clem Everett stepped down from the dust-caked stagecoach outside the Wells Fargo office and stood like a statue as people moved back and forth along the busy street. The shotgun guard handed the small canvas bag from the roof of the coach into the marshal's hands.

Everett touched the brim of his Stetson and started walking along the boardwalk in the direction of his house.

With every step he thought about the Valko Kid.

Was it possible for him to convince the young wanted man that he should turn his back on the peaceful existence that he had known for the past two years?

Could even a pardon from the governor persuade Valko?

Clem Everett opened the white gate and strolled up to the house that he had lived in for almost ten years. He paused as his fingers searched for his keys and studied the once welcoming building. His eyes looked at the unpainted frontage as he recalled the time when it had been so very different. It had once been a home, now it was only an empty house.

He pushed the key into the lock and turned it.

Everett entered and tossed his bag on to one of the many chairs that filled the damp-smelling parlour. He moved to the circular table, picked up a box of matches and then lit the wick of the oil-lamp at its centre. The marshal turned the small brass wheel until the flame was a mere inch high. He placed a cracked glass bowl over it and then sighed heavily.

The lamplight danced on the small photographic image in the silver frame on top of the mantelpiece. He moved to it as he had done for the previous three years and looked at the yellowing image of his late wife.

'Mary!' He sighed regretfully.

He knew that he had spent far too much time away from her chasing outlaws across Texas for the price on their heads to ever be a good husband. So much time that he had not even known when she had become ill. His entire body shook when he remembered how shocked he had been when he had returned to find that she had died and had been lying in her grave for nearly five weeks.

'I'm so sorry, Mary.'

Clem Everett had lost the only thing that he had ever cared about. He had not even known that anything was wrong. He cursed himself for that.

He pulled a cigar from his pocket, bit off its tip, gripped it in his teeth and leant over the lamp. The funnelled heat from the lamp ignited the long length of hand-rolled Havana tobacco. He inhaled deeply and then looked at the face in the picture again.

It looked little like the woman he had loved.

She had been so colourful and this image was faded. His fingers touched the glass as he desperately tried to see her face in his mind.

To recall the way she really looked.

Then Everett realized that he could not. He had left her alone in this house so many times over the years that when he had been here, he had not even looked at her properly.

He had taken her for granted as so many people do. It had never even dawned on him that she might not be here one day when he returned after leading yet another posse.

The cigar fell from his mouth and hit the floor at his feet. He placed one of his boots on to it and crushed it.

If he could no longer remember what she looked like, was she gone for ever?

He straightened up, moved to the closest chair and opened his canvas bag. He hauled the trail shirt and pants from it and changed out of the fancy clothes. Everett was not going to sleep in this empty shell of a house tonight, he thought. He might never return to it.

There was work to do. Important work. He would ride through the night to reach the place where he knew he would find the young man whom he regarded as the fastest gun alive.

Within minutes the marshal had left the house and was headed for the livery stable. He buttoned up his heavy hip-length coat and fished his trail gloves from its pockets. He stretched the kid leather over his hands until they were like a second skin. Lantern-light snaked across the dusty streets from almost every building as he headed for the stables. Everett aimed his pointed high-heeled boots straight at the tall wooden building. He spied the blacksmith sitting on his anvil near the open doorway, sucking on a pipe.

'Get my horse ready, Olaf. Will ya?'

The large owner of the livery got to his feet.

'It's kinda late for you to be going out riding, ain't it, Marshal?'

'Reckon you might be right,' Everett agreed. He followed the burly figure into the interior of the lantern-lit stables, 'but sometimes there ain't no choice. I've got me someone to see.'

The livery man led the tall brown gelding from its stall and ran a huge hand along its back.

'Who ya going to see, Clem?'

Everett hauled his blanket and saddle off the top rail of the stall and walked towards his friend. He dropped the saddle on to the straw-covered floor and placed the blanket on his horse's broad back.

Dust drifted into the air as he patted the blanket down.

'You wouldn't believe me, even if I told you, Olaf.'

6

A million stars twinkled above the head of the lone rider as he steered his brown gelding across the high mountain trail through the pine-forest. Marshal Clem Everett had not ridden this route for more than a year but he knew every inch of the trail.

The new moon gave enough light to enable the veteran lawman to see his ultimate destination. A few miles ahead of him he could see the wooden shingles of the buildings that made up the small settlement of Dry Gulch. But it was not the town itself that the marshal was heading for.

His objective was a small ranch set between the trees and the group of wooden buildings.

Clem Everett had ridden all night to reach this place before dawn. He had made good time and knew that he would arrive at least an hour before sunrise.

The long-legged horse gathered pace as it made its way out of the fragrant trees and along the dusty trail which led to the sleeping Dry Gulch.

Everett's eyes narrowed as he stared through the bluish moonlight at the town. The entire town was in darkness. He thought about the contrast between this place and Waco. It seemed that the bigger the town, the less people slept. The saloons and gaming-halls never closed their doors to potential business in Waco or other similarly sized places.

Dry Gulch was asleep.

The lawman liked that.

A half-mile after he had left the forest, Everett spotted the well-hidden turning to his left. Dry grass reached almost six feet in height across the dirt track. He eased back on his reins and stopped the horse.

Dust filtered through the dry night air as the horseman steadied his mount. He pulled the reins to his left and allowed the tired creature beneath his saddle to face the seldom-used trail.

'The trail has sure gotten itself overgrown. I almost missed it, Blue,' Clem Everett said to his lathered-up horse. He leant forward and ran a gloved hand down its neck.

Everett stood in his stirrups in a vain attempt see the ranch house that he knew was a quarter-mile ahead of him. Overhanging tree-branches almost touched the ground and a wall of grass tried to reach the sky.

The ranch house beyond was hidden from everyone except those who actually knew that it was there at all.

The lawman urged his tired horse forward and through the natural barricade. The long-legged creature moved cautiously through the high grass.

Everett continued riding until eventually he saw the small ranch house set beneath the canopies of two large oak trees. Even the moonlight seemed incapable of penetrating the dense foliage of the massive branches. To the left of the house he could just make out a barn. There was no light escaping from either of the wooden structures. He pulled back on his reins and slowed the gelding to walking pace. Then he stopped and just studied the area carefully.

He had not been to this place for nearly two years. Not since he had brought the unconscious Valko here after finding him beside his powerful white stallion. A few hours earlier the Kid had nobly left him in the high mountain town of Bear Claw, to vainly trail his evil impostor.

Everett had repaid his debt that night.

The Valko Kid had saved his life but it had almost cost him his own. The marshal had known that the youngster was far more seriously injured than the Kid would admit. He had used his tracking skills to follow at a discreet distance until he had seen Valko fall from his saddle.

By that time they were far nearer the

small town of Dry Gulch than the busy Bear Claw.

Everett dismounted and stood beside his horse.

He remembered taking Valko to the doctor's home and remaining until the Kid had regained consciousness. Then he had asked a big favour of his old friend Sheriff Tom Clyde.

He had said that Valko was his nephew, Roy Edwards, and needed a place to recover from injuries he had suffered riding with his posse. The sheriff had led them to the deserted old ranch house before which he now stood.

After a week, Everett had left the young wanted man with enough money to buy provisions for a few weeks. He had told Clyde to write each month and give him reports of Valko's progress.

The old sheriff had done exactly that.

Everett knew that Valko had managed to fend for himself in Dry Gulch. He earned a little by helping other ranchers with their stock as well as doing odd jobs around the town. He had been accepted and eventually managed to find a place where he no longer had to use his matched Colts. Few of the people in and around Dry Gulch had even heard of the Valko Kid and none would have believed that the handsome young man they knew as Roy Edwards could possibly be a notorious outlaw.

Sheriff Tom Clyde had told Everett that for more than a year the young man had not even worn his guns. He began to wonder whether even the promise of a pardon from the governor could make the Kid leave this quiet sanctuary.

Everett led his tired horse closer to the house. There was no sign of life in it. He started to wonder if Valko might have left and found himself another safe haven.

Everett strode through the long grass and looked into the barn. He squinted hard and then saw the large powerful white stallion standing in his stall. He sighed with relief as the white horse nodded its noble head up and down. He knew the affection that the Kid had for the handsome animal. Its sheer strength had managed to save the kid's life on countless occasions as it managed to keep ahead of one posse after another. Valko had risked his own life by refusing to abandon the stallion when it was injured, and waiting for the creature's wounds to heal.

'I reckon Valko must be here if you are, big fella,' Everett whispered to the horse, stroking its neck. 'He'd not go anywhere without you, would he?'

Suddenly Marshal Clem Everett heard the sound of a gun being cocked. Before he could move a muscle he felt its cold steel barrel touching his neck just below his right ear.

'Reach for the sky, stranger!' said a voice from out of the shadows.

7

A rooster crowed as Marshal Clem Everett turned his head slowly towards the voice he recognized. The smile on the face of the Valko Kid was illuminated in the first rays of the rising sun. The lawman exhaled heavily as he watched the young man lower the weapon and tuck it into his belt.

'Valko!'

'Roy Edwards,' the Kid corrected.

'Is that what the folks around here call you, son?'

'Yep.'

'Is it your real name?' Everett was curious.

Valko shrugged. 'Might be. But then again I just might have been christened Valko. It don't matter none.'

The marshal stepped closer to the young man.

'Reckon fewer folks shoot at Roy

Edwards though.'

'That's right. Lead does kinda seek Valko out more than most other handles.' Valko grinned as he looked at the still pale lawman. 'Are you OK, Marshal?'

'You scared the life out of me,' Everett admitted, removing his Stetson and wiping the sweat from his brow with the tails of his bandanna.

Valko touched the gun grip.

'Don't fret. It ain't even loaded. There ain't no call even to have a gun in these parts.'

'I never even heard you come out of the house, son.' The lawman started to walk beside the slightly shorter Kid towards the house.

'That's because I was out back feeding the chickens.' Valko stepped up on to the porch and opened the front door of the small ranch house. He led the marshal into a neat room. 'I get up darn early these days. I've got a little stock and they like being fed before the rooster crows.'

Everett sat down on a hardback chair and rested his right elbow on the table. He could barely believe the change in the Kid since he had last set eyes on him.

'You seem settled here, Kid.'

The Valko Kid opened the curtains and allowed the light into the room. He then struck a match, dropped it into the small stove and placed a blackened coffee-pot on its cast-iron top. The dry kindling inside the ancient stove warmed the air of the cool room.

'I never had the chance to thank you, Marshal.'

'There was no need, son. I owed you.'

Valko nodded and sat down opposite the man who had once spent a year of his life leading a posse after him.

'Am I still worth twenty-five thousand bucks?'

'Yep. Dead or alive.' Everett placed his hat on his knee and looked at the younger man's face. It was a healthy face which beamed colour. He recalled how different that face had looked the last time he had been with the Kid.

'And you must be darn close to retirement, Marshal. You ain't come to collect, have you?' There was an anxious tone as Valko looked straight at the man who had somehow become a friend.

'Nope.' Everett grinned.

'Then why are you here?' Valko toyed with the crumbs on top of the otherwise clean table. 'I reckon a man like you don't waste his time visiting folks. Why are you here?'

The lawman knew that the Kid's instinct for survival was still as sharp as ever. In turn, Valko sensed that something was bothering the marshal.

'I never met anyone quite like you, son. All my years chasing outlaws and then I meet you.' Everett was staring at the floor as he spoke. 'Two years ago I was ready to kill you like a cornered rat. Ready to claim that reward. Then I come up against the varmint who stole your life away from you. He kills most of my posse and gets the drop on me. You saved my life and nearly got yourself killed. You're a pretty special man, Kid.'

'You ain't answered my question, Marshal.'

'The name's Clem Everett, Valko. Call me Clem.'

Valko leaned back in his chair and bit his lower lip thoughtfully. He smiled.

'You still ain't answered my question, Clem.'

Everett looked up and into the face of the man opposite him.

'I've been given a real hard job by the Governor himself. It could ruin Texas if I get it wrong.'

Valko listened silently.

Everett continued: 'I have to track down a gang of deadly outlaws and get a darn important document back. I've only just over a week left to get this done, Valko.'

'Carry on,' said the Kid.

'There ain't no way that I can go up against them on my own, son. I just ain't got the gun skills. I need your help.' The marshal had not taken his eyes from Valko once as he explained. 'Will you help me?'

The Kid rose back to his feet and checked the coffee-pot.

'You're asking a lot, Clem.'

Everett stood up and moved to the side of the Kid.

'I know, Kid. I would never ask you to help me if this wasn't so darn important. You've got yourself a life here. I'm asking you to ride back into a life that you've managed to quit. But the Governor said that if you did help me, he'd give you a pardon.'

Valko's eyes flashed up at the older man.

'A pardon?'

'Yep.' Everett rested his hand on the kid's shoulder. 'A pardon. You'd be a free man. You'd not have to hide anymore.'

The Valko Kid pulled two tin cups off a shelf and rested them of the top of the stove.

'I'd be a free man?'

'Yep.' Everett watched Valko hard.

The Kid moved to the window and stared out at the land that he had tended for more than a year.

'How many of them in this gang, Clem?'

'Eight.'

Valko shook his head. 'How many others have you enlisted?'

'No one. I figured that it would be best if there were just the two of us.'

'Who stole that document, Clem? Who led the gang?'

'Black Bill Bodie,' came the reply.

Valko tilted his head and looked at the marshal.

'Black Bill is fast, Clem. Damn fast.'

'That's why I need you. Only you could out draw that varmint, son,' Everett said.

'You don't need me, Clem.'

'I do, Kid!' exclaimed Everett.

'I'm just a guy with a few chickens and a milk cow. I'm Roy Edwards.'

Clem Everett felt his heart sink.

'What you saying, son?'

The younger man turned and stood squarely in front of the US marshal. He shrugged and pointed at the hand-tooled gunbelt and holsters hanging on a hook near the door. He pulled the gun from his belt and dropped it into the empty holster.

'You need the Valko Kid.'

Everett watched as the Kid pulled the belt down and wrapped it around his hips. He buckled it and then started to load the guns silently.

'Are you gonna help me or not?'

Valko twirled both his guns until they slid into their holsters. It had been a long time since he had done that and he was pleased that he still could.

'Reckon I have to help you, Clem. I owe you. Besides, I can't let you go up against Bodie and his gang alone. He'd kill you faster than I can spit.'

The marshal felt a lump in his throat.

'We might not live through this one, Valko. Bodie is bad enough but he has seven deadly outlaws riding with him.'

The Valko Kid nodded.

'Pour the coffee, Clem. I ain't going nowhere until I've had me some breakfast.'

'Then you're going to help me?'

Valko nodded again.

'Yep.'

8

As Clem Everett sat finishing off his breakfast at Valko's table he recalled that he had been given one more vital piece of information before leaving Austin. He reached into his shirt-pocket and pulled out the folded sheet of paper. The Governor's secretary Jacob Francis had arrived at the luxurious hotel rooms an hour before the US marshal was due to check out and head back to Waco.

The marshal wondered why he had not thought anything about it until this moment. Why he had accepted the added information without question.

Francis had handed Everett an unsealed envelope containing a brief note. At the bottom of the brief message, Sloane had signed his name. The message read,

Dear Marshal Everett,

Although I have been unable to let you see the original letter from Bill Bodie, due to its delicate contents, I can let you know that he asked for a ransom of $100,000 in gold or he will go south of the border and sell the document to the Mexican government. Bodie will be at Devil's Peak on the 17th.

Yours
Hyram Sloane.

The lawman stared at the crumpled note in his hand, then flattened it out. His wrinkled eyes read it again silently.

'What you got there, Clem?' asked the Kid.

'Good question, son,' Everett replied. He handed the note to the Valko Kid. He watched as the younger man read it carefully.

'Who is this Sloane character?' Valko asked.

'He's the Governor, Kid.'

'I never heard of the critter.'

Valko finished his breakfast, then returned the sheet of paper to his friend. He had a strange look on his face as he rose and placed the dishes in a bucket of soapy water. 'You ever been to Devil's Peak, Clem?'

'Nope. I've heard of it though. Why?'

Valko rested a boot on his chair and tied his leather holster laces around his thighs.

'I've been there twice. Both times I got myself bushwhacked.'

Everett mopped up the egg-yoke on his tin plate with a bread-crust, then leaned back in his chair and studied the Kid.

'I don't like the sound of that.'

'Bodie has chosen this place because it gives the advantage to the hunter and not the hunted,' Valko explained. 'To reach Devil's Peak, you have to ride through a valley with solid rock walls. A hundred feet high in places. Good cover for anyone hiding on the rockfaces. Eight men could massacre an army there without losing a single gunhand.'

Clem Everett rose and dropped his plate into the bucket, then moved to the open window. He inhaled the crisp morning air.

'A trap?'

Valko shrugged.

'Could be. When did Sloane give you this letter?'

'He didn't,' Everett said thoughtfully. 'His private secretary brought it to my hotel room just before I headed back for Waco.'

'Did Sloane mention any of this?'

The taller man turned.

'Come to think about it, he didn't mention anything that's in that letter.'

'Nothing about the ransom or Devil's Peak?' Valko rubbed his jawline.

'Nope. He just told me to try to enlist your help and go get that valuable document back. He said that I had the authority to hang Black Bill and his men though.'

The Valko Kid led his friend out into the sunshine and towards the barn.

'I don't like this.'

'What's going on, Kid?' Everett asked as he caught up to the brooding younger man. 'What are you thinking?'

'I'm thinking that this don't add up,' Valko said. He led the magnificent white stallion out from its stall and into the warm sunshine.

Everett sat down on a tree-stump that was obviously used to chop kindling.

'You think that the Governor's secretary might have written this letter himself?'

'Yep. Maybe that's how Black Bill got wind of the document in the first place,' Valko answered. He placed the bridle over his horse's head.

'What else is worrying you, son?'

'The ransom money troubles me, Clem.'

'Why?'

''Coz Governor Sloane never said anything to you about ransom money. Right?'

'Right,' the lawman agreed.

The Kid tossed the blanket on to his

mount's back and patted it down firmly. 'But the letter doesn't say if you're to take the money to exchange for the document, Clem. If there is a ransom, who's got the money? How come Sloane didn't talk to you about that?'

'That's right, Kid.' Everett ran his fingers through his greying hair. 'Who in tarnation is meant to take the ransom to Bodie if it ain't me?'

Valko placed the heavy saddle over the stallion's broad back, then reached under its belly for the cinch straps. He tightened them.

'What's in this document anyway, Clem? What could be so valuable that it causes all this ruckus?'

'I have no idea,' the marshal admitted. 'But it's meant to be so important that it could ruin Texas.'

The Kid stared over his saddle.

'How?'

'I ain't got no idea.'

The Kid pulled the stirrup off the saddle horn and lowered the fender. He walked around the horse and rested his knuckles on his gun grips.

'This don't add up, Clem. No matter how you do the sums, this just don't add up at all. What's the name of the Governor's secretary?'

'Francis. Jacob Francis. Why?'

'Don't mean nothing to me. If he's a crook I've never heard of the critter.' Valko kicked at the ground.

'Maybe Francis ain't his real name.'

The Valko Kid nodded. 'What's he look like?'

'Like a man who has never stepped out in the sun in his entire life. If he's a crook, he's a different breed from the ones I'm used to tangling with.'

'I got me a bad feeling about this, Clem.'

The marshal rose to his feet.

'You thinking that maybe someone is setting a trap to catch the Valko Kid?' Everett suggested. 'That all this is just a lot of smoke to cover the fact that someone wants that twenty-five thousand-dollar reward on your head?'

The Kid did not reply.

'You're wrong, son. I've seen the reports from Sand Rock. Black Bill and his gang killed every living soul there. They also killed the stagecoach guard and its four passengers. This has nothing to do with some varmints trapping you. But I agree, it still smells kinda fishy.'

'What if Sloane gave the ransom to this Francis critter and he kinda forgot to hand it over to you, Clem?'

Everett loosened his bandanna and swallowed hard.

'That hadn't occurred to me, Kid. Damn, Sloane might think that I've stolen government money.'

The Kid decided to change the subject. He pointed at the marshal's fatigued mount.

'You figure that young gelding of yours is rested up enough, Clem? We got a long ride ahead of us.'

Everett shook his head.

'Hardly. I've ridden Blue all night to get here before dawn.'

'Then let's go into town and rent a saddle horse for the first part of the journey, so we can make good time to Devil's Peak,' suggested Valko. He picked up his reins from the ground and looped them over the neck of the stallion. 'You can ride one horse and rest the other.'

'But what about you? You need a spare horse as well.'

The Kid stepped into his stirrup and mounted the white horse. He patted its neck.

'Snow here is stronger than any three normal horses put together, Clem. I don't need a spare mount. He'll ride all day and night if needed.'

The lawman leaned forward and rested his wrists on his hips.

'How old is that stallion, Valko?'

'Fourteen or so.' The Kid watched his friend mount the gelding before he tapped his heels against the sides of his own horse. 'Why?'

'That's darn old for any horse,' Everett observed. He drew his gelding alongside the white stallion.

'Hush up. Snow here understands every word you say.' Valko smiled as they both headed along the overgrown track towards the road to Dry Gulch. 'He's so smart he taught me to count up to twenty without taking my boots off.'

Marshal Clem Everett laughed and looked down at the Kid's left boot in its stirrup.

'You forgot to put your spurs on, son.'

Valko glanced at the lawman.

'Never wear them.'

'I forgot.'

Both riders headed on into Dry Gulch. They picked up a spare horse, upon which the US marshal placed his well-worn saddle. He then tied the reins for his gelding to his saddle cantle. With the weight of the marshal and the heavy livery off the horse's back, the lawman knew that even being led along the trail, his prized Blue would be rested by late afternoon.

The Valko Kid led the way. The riders headed into the pine covered hills.

It would take a lot of hard riding to reach Devil's Peak.

9

The noonday sun burned down ferociously across every inch of the vast Lone Star State. It was hotter than the bowels of hell and few sane men ventured out beneath its merciless rays. San Cortez was a small town, just three miles east of El Paso, which reflected its Latin origins more than most. Most of its buildings were whitewashed adobes with red-tiled roofs, like those south of the border in Mexico. Only the telegraph office and feed store bore any similarity to Texan architecture. In other respects San Cortez was unlike its far larger neighbour. It was relatively quiet and free from anything resembling the law. This was why it attracted outlaws like flies to a ripe garbage pail. They knew that San Cortez was just a short ride from El Paso and the bountiful pleasures which that sprawling metropolis offered those with the time and money to indulge themselves.

Even the Texas Rangers avoided San Cortez.

Black Bill Bodie stood in the telegraph office and accepted the reply slip from the small bespectacled man. The outlaw looked at the pencilled writing and then gave a satisfied grunt. He fumbled in his vest pocket, produced a silver dollar and tossed it into the man's hands.

'Buy yourself some vittles, partner,' Bodie mocked. 'You look like you need a good feed.'

He turned and walked out of the open doorway into the bright street and inhaled deeply. His half-closed eyes wrinkled up as he grinned and waved the crushed note in his hand at Grange.

'Got it, Frankie boy! The news we bin waiting for.'

Frank Grange was holding both their horses as the larger man descended the three wooden steps to the dusty street.

He handed Black Bill's reins to the outlaw leader and both men mounted their horses. Each of them rose off the hot leather and balanced in their stirrups until their shadows cooled the saddle seats.

'How come we had to wait here nearly all day for that message, Bill? My skin's almost burned right off. The rest of the boys must have drunk that cantina dry by now.'

'You'll get drunk enough before sundown.'

'I sure hope so!'

Black Bill Bodie lowered himself, pulled at his reins and turned his pinto stallion's head until the horse was facing the wide, sun-drenched street. There were few other people bold enough or stupid enough to venture out at noon. He screwed up his eyes against the bright sunlight until they appeared to be closed.

He steadied his mount.

'You sure are dumb, Frank. Dumb but as loyal as an old hound dog.'

'I ain't gonna argue with you none,' Grange said, turning his own horse around. 'I'm too thirsty to spit, let alone confab.'

Bodie held the small slip of paper in his dirty right hand and waved it under the nose of his most trustworthy follower.

'This is important information, Frankie. This is from my powerful friend in Austin. It tells me what we gotta do next.' Grange tried to focus on the paper.

'It does?'

'Yep.' Black Bill kicked the spur on his left boot back and felt his stallion buck forward beneath him. He stood up in his stirrups and allowed the large animal to canter down the street with Grange at his right elbow.

'I thought you were making the decisions.'

Bodie nodded.

'I am, you loco bean. But this is bigger than just a simple robbery and the like. This job is hotter than a ripe chilli pepper. The man that planned this is mighty important. I'm just the executer of his plans. He thinks I'm gonna do everything he tells me.'

'But I thought that we was going south to Mexico to sell that fancy document, Bill?'

'We are.' Bodie nodded. 'But first we gotta head to Devil's Peak.'

'How come?'

Bodie's cruel eyes darted at his companion.

'Because there's a hundred thousand dollars in gold coin being delivered there by a certain Marshal Clem Everett in a few days' time. We're meant to hand over the document for the gold. That's when I change my friend's plans. We'll have the money and the document.'

'Huh?' Grange could not hide his confusion at the best of times, and his confusion at the words which greeted him from the hardened outlaw emphasized his unbridled stupidity. 'We gonna get paid for something?'

'Stop thinkin', Frank,' Bodie commanded. 'You ain't designed to think.'

Grange's head rocked back and forth as he chuckled. It was like looking at a jackass in more ways than one, thought Bodie.

'Do we have to tell the rest of the boys?'

'Yep,' answered Black Bill Bodie bluntly. 'We have to tell them, Frank.'

'Why?' Frank Grange had no loyalty to anyone except the powerful man riding beside him. 'I figure that we don't need Sam and Jett and the others to collect that hundred thousand dollars. One marshal don't take much killing. Heck, I could do it on my own.'

'I need the extra guns, Frank.'

'How come?'

''Coz this message tells me that my first plan has to be changed a tad.' Black Bill explained. 'My friend in Austin tells me that the marshal is bringing a top gun with him.'

'Ain't nobody faster than you, Black Bill,' Frank Grange said. 'Who is he bringing with him, anyway?'

Black Bill Bodie hesitated for a second before he looked across at the buck-toothed face.

'The Valko Kid!'

The smile evaporated from Frank Grange's lips.

'Valko?'

Bodie nodded and spat at the ground. He continued to stab his spurs into his pinto's flesh.

'Yep! Valko! And he's said to be fast. Damn fast.'

Both horsemen continued until they reached the small whitewashed cantina. The six mounts of their fellow gang members were tied up outside.

Bodie pulled back until his pinto stallion stopped, then he dismounted quickly. He tied his reins to the horn of Sam Baker's saddle and walked around the line of flicking tails to the cantina's beaded curtain. Black Bill pulled out a half-cigar from his vest pocket and placed it between his yellow teeth. He fumbled for a match and ran his thumb nail across it. Black Bill cupped the flame to the end of the short, twisted weed and inhaled deeply.

He rested his hands on the gun grips of his Remington .44s as Grange slid to the ground.

'Why do we need the rest of the boys, Bill?'

Bodie leaned over and whispered into the outlaw's ear.

'Cannon fodder, Frank. Cannon fodder.'

10

Hyram Sloane walked along the marble corridor of the Governor's mansion and entered the smoke-filled room at its end. He closed the doors behind him and turned to face the figure seated next to the wide-open french windows.

Sloane walked silently across the deep-carpeted room until he was directly beside the man with the pipe gripped firmly between his teeth. He sighed heavily.

'General!'

The army officer looked up at the strained features of the man who, it was claimed, was the most powerful in Texas. General Tiberius Jackson knew the truth. For it was he who controlled the armed forces in Texas and that made *him* the most powerful man in the Lone Star State.

'Afternoon, Hyram.'

'What are you doing here, General?'

'I'm here because you need me, Hyram.' Jackson tapped the pipe-bowl on the heel of his boot and smiled as the burning tobacco landed on the expensive carpet.

The Governor rubbed the smouldering ashes underfoot and then stepped out into the shade of the enormous garden. Sloane stared around the well-kept gardens and loosened his stiff collar with his finger.

He inhaled the heavy scent of the countless varieties of roses which were planted in every spare plot of ground behind the mansion and listened to the chair creaking behind him.

The heavy military boots squeaked as the general walked out and stood shoulder to shoulder beside him.

'My spies tell me things, Hyram. Many things. Things that your people think that they can hide from me. But they cannot hide anything from Tiberius Jackson. I've been in Austin longer than most of the buildings. And I pay my spies well. That is why I have held this position for such a very long time.'

'You're talking in riddles, General.'

'Indeed. That is my way. I have been in Austin for such a long time that I have been infected by your illness.'

Sloane's eyes darted at the barrel-chested man who wore his military ribbons like a shield.

'What illness?'

'I have contracted politics.' Jackson's laughter was subdued like his voice. 'A malady that I fear is fatal. I shall never give a straight answer to a simple question again, I fear.'

Sloane turned his head. His face was red.

'Why are you here?'

'I have heard a rumour.'

The Governor cleared his throat.

'Get to the point, General.'

'It seems that you have mislaid something.' Jackson watched the beads of sweat trickle down the colourless face.

'What have I mislaid?' Sloane asked evasively.

'Don't be silly, Hyram. You have lost a certain document, have you not?' Jackson began to walk. He stepped off the flagstones and on to the close-mowed grass lawn, a lawn that was bigger than most public parks in the city.

Hyram Sloane followed.

'Who told you this?'

'A spy.'

'Give me his name.'

'So it is true, Hyram.' There was a certain sound in the voice of the army man. It was the sound of satisfaction. 'I thought so. My spies are never wrong.'

'I have made arrangements to ensure its return.' Sloane said as he caught up with Jackson. 'No one will be any the wiser. I shall have it back in its vault by the twentieth.'

Jackson stopped and turned. He stared hard into the softer, less weathered face.

'If you do not, it will mean ruin for you.'

Sweat began to trickle down the side of the bald man's head like rain.

'Why are you here, Tiberius? To gloat? I do not like being mocked by anyone.'

'No, Hyram. You misunderstand my motives. I am here to help you resolve this to both our satisfactions.'

'How? Why?'

The military officer rested a hand on the troubled politician's shoulder. It was a long time since he had been on a battlefield but he had lost none of his cunning.

'I have people who can and will act on my behalf. Call them agents or whatever. They do as I order. You ask why I would help you, Hyram? Well, you might not be my favourite person, but you are a man who can and will repay his debts. Am I correct?'

Sloane nodded. 'But I've sent a man to get the document back, General. A loyal Texan. A man whom I feel I can trust.'

'Marshal Clem Everett?'

'Yes.'

'A fine man. A good choice. But I think that you do not realize that there are others in this government who are working against you, Hyram.' Jackson placed the pipe between his teeth again and chewed on its stem. 'What about the ransom money?'

'What ransom money?' Sloane's expression could not hide his confusion. 'I've not had any demands for money.'

'You have.' General Jackson corrected. 'But it did not reach you. It was intercepted.'

Sloane ran his fingers over his face.

'I do not understand.'

'Jacob Francis took a note purporting to be from you to Everett before he returned to Waco.' Jackson told him. 'The note mentioned the ransom of a hundred thousand dollars in gold.'

'I know nothing of this.'

Jackson sighed heavily. 'That's because this entire thing has been the brainchild of Francis. It was he who informed Black Bill Bodie of the document's route. He also managed to fake your signature on the note and a few other things as well.'

'Then I'll issue a warrant for his arrest immediately.'

'He's gone.'

'What?'

'And so has a hundred thousand dollars in gold coin from the treasury.'

Hyram Sloane felt his knees buckle.

'What can I do, Tiberius?'

'You will let me act on your behalf, Hyram.'

General Jackson led the stunned politician further away from the mansion and tried to explain.

11

Black Bill Bodie walked into the cantina and straight towards the six outlaws propped against the wooden bar counter. Seeing his fearsome reflection in the long mirror behind the bartender, his drunken men parted like the Red Sea a few seconds before he reached them.

'Whiskey!' Bodie snarled.

The man behind the wet bar grabbed the best-looking whiskey bottle and handed it to the outlaw leader.

'Howdy, Mr Bodie,' the man croaked, like a frightened frog.

'Frank'll pay you, sonny,' Bodie said. He grabbed the neck of the bottle and wandered towards one of the busy tables. He stared down at the four seated men. 'Move out, partners. I'm sitting there.'

One of the seated drinkers looked up.

He studied the two crossed ammunition belts and the face that glared down at him with a total disregard for his own safety.

'You talking to us, you ugly bastard?'

Black Bill lowered his head until his eyes were fixed on the loud-mouthed man. He smiled.

'You other men as dumb as him?'

The three other drinkers rose and moved away from the table quickly. The talkative fourth remained seated and staring at Bodie.

'Just because you're carrying more bullets than an army pack-mule, don't mean that I'm scared of you, old-timer.'

Bodie's seven men all looked at one another in total amazement. They had never heard anyone talk to Black Bill that way and it amused them.

'Reckon we got ourselves a frisky one, Bill.' Sam Baker laughed as he rubbed his empty eyesocket with his thumb.

Jett Clooney edged forward.

'He's either drunk or loco, Bill.'

Black Bill Bodie placed the bottle on top of the table and stared down at the man, who continued to drink.

'Which one is it, mister? You stupid or just drunk?'

'Go away. I hate old-timers who just can't come to grips with the fact that they've lived too long. Way too long.'

Bodie straightened up. His fingers flexed above the handles of his .44s.

'I don't like killing folks in this town. Kinda makes the rest of the population upset.'

The man lowered his whiskey glass from his lips.

'I ain't from here. I'm from Dodge City. You heard of Dodge City?'

Bodie grinned.

'Draw!'

Before the man could say or do anything, he saw the hands of the notorious outlaw pull both his weapons from their holsters and aim at his head. The man was no coward and remained seated as he looked past the gun barrels at the grim-faced Bodie.

'You trying to scare me, old-timer?'

'Nope,' replied Black Bill. 'I ain't trying to scare you at all. I'm just trying to kill you.'

The seated man's right hand dropped to his holster and attempted to pull the Colt out.

'You ain't killing me!'

'Wrong!' Both barrels of Bodie's Remingtons blasted at exactly the same time. The noise bounced off the adobe walls of the cantina as the man's limp body was torn apart by the point-blank shots.

Every eye within the cantina watched as the man's chair was knocked backwards by the force of the simultaneous shots. A trail of blood hung in the gunsmoke filled air as the body crashed on to the floor.

'You killed him, Bill,' muttered Frank Grange from the bar as he took his first sip of whiskey.

Bodie glanced around the cantina.

'Yep. I killed him OK, Frankie.'

'Reckon you taught him a lesson

there, Bill.' Grange chuckled wryly.

Black Bill looked at the wide-eyed stare on the dead man's face as the body lay on its back in the filthy sawdust-covered floor. The two bullets had blown a massive hole in the middle of the body.

'Yep. He learned to respect his elders the hard way.'

Jett Clooney went to sit down at the table when he felt a gun barrel tap his arm. He looked into Bodie's face.

'What? I thought we was sitting down. I thought that's why you shot the big-mouth, Bill.'

Bodie holstered his guns.

'I ain't sitting there to do my drinking, Jett.'

'How come?' Clooney asked drunkenly.

'Half his guts are covering the damn table.' Black Bill roared with laughter. 'Reckon I'll drink my whiskey at the bar instead. I ain't an animal, am I?'

12

The next two days saw the temperature rise steadily. The Valko Kid galloped up the steep incline, with Clem Everett a dozen or more yards behind the tail of the white stallion. The two riders had covered a lot of ground in the previous two days and were exhausted.

The Kid hauled his reins back.

'Easy, Snow.'

The large horse stopped and snorted at the ground. Valko dismounted and stood beside the shoulder of his faithful mount as the US marshal reached the flat top of the ridge astride his gelding. The lawman still had the rented saddle-horse tied to his saddlebags. He had needed to use both the horses equally to keep up with the white stallion.

Everett eased himself off his saddle and dropped to the ground. He removed his Stetson and beat the dust from it against his leg.

'Don't that horse of yours ever get tuckered out, Kid?'

Valko smiled.

'That's why you could never catch me, Clem.'

Both men dropped their hats on to the ground and watered the three mounts. The Kid licked his dry lips and moved to the edge of the ridge. He stared down at the strange, barren landscape. He had been here before and it troubled him.

'What you thinking, Valko?' Everett asked.

'I'm thinking that we might be biting off more than either of us can chew, Clem,' the Kid freely admitted, resting his wrists on his gun grips.

'I've never been here before.' The lawman stared down into the heat haze which curled the air and made it almost impossible to see anything clearly. 'But it sure looks hostile down there.'

The Kid rubbed the dust from his

face and pointed.

'Devil's Peak is over in that direction.'

The marshal screwed up his eyes and tried to see the infamous rock, but could not make it out.

'I'll have to take your word for it.'

Valko exhaled heavily, pointed down to a deep canyon to their right. Black shadows ensured that neither man could make out what lay down there in the depths of the chasm.

'If my memory serves me right, there's a deserted cabin half-way down there, Clem. I used that to rest up for a few days once when a posse had almost run me into the ground.'

'Could we use it tonight?'

Valko nodded.

'It has water and half a roof, as I recall.'

'I figure we made good time getting here because you knew of that short cut from Dry Gulch,' Everett admitted. 'We must have a day to spare by my reckoning.'

The Valko Kid frowned and turned away from the blindingly sun-drenched land below their high vantage point. He plucked his hat from the ground and placed it over his dark hair. Droplets of sweat ran down the side of his face as he leaned against the powerful stallion.

'Black Bill might be there already for all we know.'

'Is there another way to reach Devil's Peak that don't require us riding through that valley you told me about, Kid?' Everett could not conceal his concern. A concern which he knew was also worrying his young friend.

Valko lifted his head from the saddle and turned to look at the lawman.

'The only other way is for us to skim the very edge of that mountain range over yonder. That would take us to almost half-way up the peak itself. I ain't ever heard of anyone being loco enough to try it though.'

The US marshal rubbed his chin.

'Is it possible for horses to negotiate that route?'

Valko shrugged and bit his lower lip.
'I'm not sure.'
'I'm willing to try it if you are, son.'
'Reckon it might give us a better chance than riding through the valley itself.' Valko sighed. 'We could end up getting behind Bodie and his gang.'
Everett bent over and picked his hat off the dusty ground. He tapped it and then slid it over his grey hair.
'Better than being a sitting duck.'
Valko gathered up his reins and held the saddle horn firmly in his left hand. He hopped up and placed his left boot into the stirrup. He threw his right leg over the stallion's back.
'C'mon. We'll head for that cabin before it gets dark,' satd Valko, as the marshal mounted the gelding. 'We need water and rest if we're gonna try and teach these horses to climb a mountain in the morning, Clem.'
The distant sound of gunshots rang out from the land below the two mounted men. Both men rose in their saddles and tried to make out from

where it had originated.

'What you reckon, Kid?'

Valko eased Snow closer to the edge of the ridge and looked all around the sun-bleached landscape. He was just about to speak when he caught a glimpse of dust rising from behind a jagged white line of rocks. The dust hung on the dry air.

He pointed. 'There! See it, Clem?'

'I see it.'

'Riders!' Valko added. 'Only horses could kick up that much dust.'

'Black Bill and his gang?' Everett queried.

'It can't be. Not from that direction.' Valko was puzzled as he looked at the lawman and then back down at the trail dust as it grew longer and longer. 'Whoever that is, they're coming from the north.'

'How far away do you figure they are?'

'Twenty miles or so from here.' Valko ran his hand along the neck of his eager stallion. 'But they're headed for Devil's

Peak, just like us.'

Everett frowned. 'Who are they?'

'Beats me, Clem.' Valko straightened up and turned his mount away from the sheer drop. 'It can't be Bodie. Can it?'

'How many of them are there?'

'At least a few. Too much dust for just one rider.' The Kid tapped his heels against the sides of the white horse and started again for the trail which led to the cabin. 'Whoever they are, they're no closer to Devil's Peak than we are.'

Everett steered his horse towards the stallion.

'I hate to admit it, Kid, but I'm getting mighty troubled by all this.'

The Valko Kid glanced over his shoulder into his companion's frowning face.

'You ain't alone Clem.'

Both riders headed slowly down the dry dusty trail towards the shadowy canyon.

13

Satan's Pass was a valley that lived up to its name. A place that could only have been conceived in the black heartless soul of the Devil himself. A land of sand and rock where not even one blade of grass could exist. Of all the various canyons that stretched out in all directions like the legs of a spider from the massive Devil's Peak, Satan's Pass was the most dangerous. It was also the only direct route to and from the jagged golden mesa at its heart.

It was as if it had been designed to kill all those who ventured over its blisteringly hot sand. The high walls on both sides made it a perfect place to ambush unsuspecting riders. Yet Satan's Pass did not require men with guns or rifles to kill unwanted intruders. There was no water here that any human had ever been able to find. The platoon of twenty seasoned riders had come a long way since they had received the telegraph message from Austin.

It was nearly forty miles from the Texas Rangers' most northerly outpost at Crawford's Drift to the desolate sun-baked land which surrounded the notorious natural mesa called Devil's Peak.

Major Ethan Clark had known that few creatures willingly chose to live in this burning place. Only diamondback rattlers and countless types of deadly lizards could exist in the ferocious heat, which never eased up.

The gunsmoke still hung on the dry air as the major stared down at the headless rattlesnake which lay a few yards ahead of his mount.

'Who fired that shot?' Clark asked, looking over his shoulder at the faces of his men.

Sergeant Buck Macready shrugged and holstered his gun.

'Sorry, Major. I thought that critter was gonna sink them fangs of his into the legs of your hoss.'

The Texas Ranger officer slapped his thigh in frustrated anger. He had wanted to enter this land unseen and unheard. He knew that the sound of a gun being discharged would resonate throughout the acrid land.

'You damn fool, Buck. I wanted to get to Devil's Peak without anyone knowing of our presence here. Now everything within miles will know that we're here.'

Macready shook his head. He was angry with himself.

'I'm darn sorry, Major. I just thought that you hadn't seen that rattler. He looked ready to strike. We was riding hard and fast and kicking up a whole lotta dust.'

Clark dismounted and gestured for his platoon to do the same.

'Let's make camp. There ain't much light left and we're all dog-tired.'

'Can we make a fire, sir?' asked a voice from the group of men.

'Nope. Cold rations tonight, men.

Water the horses and grab yourselves a can of beans out of your saddlebags. Remember, we are on a secret mission. We have to get to Devil's Peak without anyone knowing we are here.'

The Texas Rangers could see the concern in the face of the man who had earned his officer's rank the hard way. If Major Ethan Clark was troubled, they knew that they all had reason to be anxious.

'Get them saddles off the backs of these animals, boys,' Buck Macready added. 'Tie your reins to them good and tight. That'll stop these nags wandering off during the night. Remember, boys, if you lose your hoss, then you'll be walking back to Crawford's Drift.'

Clark walked towards Macready.

'Sorry, Buck.'

'For what, sir?'

'Bawling you out in front of the men. I'm just a tad nervous of this place. It ain't like anywhere else I've ever had the misfortune to visit.'

Macready knelt down and ran his hand across the hot sand.

'Even the Apaches quit living here, Major. What are we doing here? What's so damn important about us reaching Devil's Peak, anyway?'

Clark knelt down beside his sergeant. He lowered his voice so that his words were only heard by the man beside him.

'All I know is that Colonel Thomas had a wire from somebody in Austin. We have to get to Devil's Peak and help a US marshal recover a document.'

'Recover it from whom?'

'Outlaws.'

'These outlaws got names, Major?'

'Black Bill is the leader, Buck.'

'Bodie?' Macready felt his throat go dry. 'We're going up against Black Bill Bodie?'

'I'm afraid so.' Clark sighed heavily.

'But why?' Macready was no coward but he was not a man to relish suicide, either. He knew the reputation of the infamous Bodie. It was something he did not wish to test.

'I'm not sure. The whole thing is very mysterious, Buck. But orders are orders.'

Buck Macready stood and looked around them. The walls of the valley were high. Far too high for his liking. Sweat ran down his face as he walked toward the seven-foot-long body of the snake. He plucked it off the sand and tossed it into the rocks.

'How many men has Bodie got with him, sir?'

'A half-dozen, or so I'm told,' Clark replied.

Macready's eyes narrowed. 'That's too many guns for these young boys to tackle, Major. Most of these boys are still wet behind their ears. They ain't got no fighting experience like us. Black Bill's deadly on his own but with that many guns at his side, our platoon will be slaughtered.'

'That's why we were meant to get to Devil's Rock without anyone knowing about it.' Clark pulled out a block of chewing tobacco from his jacket pocket and took a bite. 'But the sound of the shots might have echoed all around here off the rocks.'

Macready continued looking around the high crags of the valley walls. He was searching for any unseen enemy who might decide to use the platoon of Texas Rangers as target-practice.

'If Bodie and his gang are already here someplace, they might not be able to work out where my shots came from. With any luck, my shots will have seemed to come from somewhere else in the god-forsaken land, Major.'

Ethan Clark rested a hand on the older man's shoulder.

'I pray that you're right, Buck.'

'You and me both, sir!'

14

The Valko Kid had tried vainly to sleep for more than an hour after the sun had eventually set over the small, crumbling, wooden cabin which was perched precariously on the edge of the narrow gulch. He stared up through the large hole in the roof and watched the stars in the cloudless night sky. Valko kept having a nagging thought that would not quit. He could not get the thought of the $100,000 ransom out of his mind. Something was very wrong and yet he was unable to work out what.

His blue eyes glanced across at the snoring man beside the tiny fire they had lit in the centre of the room.

Clem Everett had fallen asleep soon after he had finished the meagre meal the Kid had prepared. The US marshal had not slept properly for days and the Kid knew it.

Valko rose to his feet and moved to the doorway. He leaned against the wall and stared hard through the moonlight at the distant chunk of rock which defiantly dominated the landscape below the cabin.

He wondered how he had managed to get into this situation.

Then he recalled how the sleeping man behind him had risked his own career in order to give him a safe place to live. The Kid always paid his debts and he owed the older man. Without Everett's timely intervention two years earlier, he would have either died or been killed. It was that simple.

Whatever doubts he secretly harboured about this confusing and dangerous mission, he knew that he had to remain at the side of the US marshal.

Valko walked out into the eerie blue moonlight to the three horses that were tied up in a line beside the cabin. He rested a hand on his stallion's neck.

'Looks like I got us into another

pickle, Snow,' he whispered into the horse's ear.

Snow nodded up and down as if answering his master.

The Kid heard movement behind him. He turned and saw the yawning Everett staggering out of the cabin.

'What's wrong, Kid?' Everett asked slowly.

'Just fretting as usual, Clem,' Valko admitted.

The lawman rested his back against the wall.

'Same here, son. I kept dreaming about that damn ransom. Woke me up.'

The two men stood close together and studied the strange yet beautiful view below them.

'I reckon we've been set up here, Valko,' Everett announced. The Kid turned his head and looked at the face of the man he had grown to respect far more than he had once considered possible.

'That's what I'm thinking. But none of it adds up. Whichever way you look at it, it still don't add up.'

'It does,' said Everett firmly, rubbing the sleep from his eyes. 'The thing is, we ain't got all the facts to look at. I reckon that someone must have hired Black Bill to steal that damn document to make the Governor look bad. Them politicians are mighty shifty characters. They all stand in a circle stabbing each other in the back. That's why there ain't no lower lifeform than damn politicians.'

'Excepting lawyers.' Valko smiled.

'Yeah. Lawyers are pretty low too,' Everett agreed. 'But I figure that something back in Austin is happening and all this is window-dressing. Sloane has to get the document back by the twentieth or he'll probably lose his job.'

Valko nodded.

'Who do you figure has the gold coin?'

'I reckon that that hundred thousand dollars ain't even left Austin, Valko,' said the marshal in a low, thoughtful tone. 'But I bet Bodie and his cohorts think it has. They'll be licking their lips and waiting for me to bring it to them.'

'Sloane must be a mighty religious man, Clem,' observed the Kid, 'if he thought that you could get the drop on Black Bill and his gang alone and string them up. And bring back the document to boot.'

Everett shrugged.

'Some men have faith.'

'How come you didn't even try to get a posse together to help you, Clem?' Valko asked.

'I did,' the lawman admitted. 'After I left the Governor's mansion I wired every top deputy that I ever rode with. When I explained to them that we were after Bodie, they all wired back refusing to help.'

'Did you tell them that I'd be riding with you?'

'Nope. I thought that that twenty-five thousand dollar bounty on your head might be a tad too tempting for some of them.'

The Valko Kid rubbed the palms of

his hands down the sides of his pants.

'I was looking at the trail that leads across the top of the ridge. We ought to be able to ride across it safe enough.'

'I think we ought to leave the quarter horse here.' Everett suggested. 'I don't want that animal spooking when its tied to my saddle.'

Valko nodded.

'You still tired?'

Everett looked up at the moon.

'Nope. I've had my fill of nightmares this night, Kid.'

'Blue and Snow look rested enough,' Valko observed. 'We could set out now and make up some time.'

Clem Everett pushed himself away from the cabin wall and grabbed his saddle horn. He hauled it up off the ground.

'Lets ride!'

15

The eight brutal horsemen had thundered for more than a mile beneath the brilliant moon across the top of the wide ridge above Satan's Pass. Black Bill Bodie hauled back on his reins and dragged his pinto stallion to a halt as his followers stopped their mounts beside him. Dust drifted into the moonlight as the outlaw leader looked around at the seven moonlit faces of his gang. The Texas Rangers' gunshots had alerted the ruthless horsemen just before sundown that they were no longer alone in the arid landscape and drawn them from their camp high in the foothills of the magnificent Devil's Peak like moths to a naked flame.

'Is this where we seen that dust rising before sundown, Frank?' Bodie asked Grange as he steadied his snorting stallion.

'It was around here someplace, Bill,' replied Grange.

Jett Clooney chewed on the leather drawstring which hung from his Stetson and stared hard into the deep valley below them. He began to get excited.

'Down there.' He pointed. 'Look down there, Bill. Do ya see them?'

'Yep. I see them.'

The six other riders peered into the valley and soon saw what their anxious companion was aiming his twitching trigger-finger at. Even in the shadows of Satan's Pass, it was still possible to see the twenty Texas Rangers and their horses.

'I like a good moon,' Sam Baker gruffed happily as he checked his hand guns. 'Even one eye can see good if'n the moon's bright enough.'

'Who are they?' Clooney questioned.

'It can't be Everett or Valko,' Bodie answered, rubbing his whiskers thoughtfully. 'Not from that direction. I'm told that Marshal Everett is headed here from Waco and Waco is over that way.

Them riders ain't come from Waco.'

'There's an awful lot of the critters, Bill,' said Grange.

'Rangers?' an outlaw called Bob Jones suggested. 'Could they be Texas Rangers?'

Black Bill sat upright in his saddle and studied the twisting canyons and valleys below their high vantage point.

'I reckon Bob is right, boys.'

Frank Grange was surprised. 'Yeah?'

'Yep. I do.' Bodie continued to aim a finger at the blue horizon. 'Them riders must have come from there. Right?'

The seven men agreed.

'And what's out there? About forty miles away?'

'Crawford's Drift?' Baker chirped up. 'Is that it?'

Bodie nodded.

'The Texas Rangers' northern outpost. Now all we gotta figure is why is a whole bunch of Texas Rangers here?'

Clooney moved his mount closer to the brooding Bodie.

'Could it be that your pal in Austin

has sent in them Texas Rangers to get us, Bill?'

'You could have been hoodwinked, Bill,' Frank Grange added.

'Maybe they come here not just to buy back that paper of yours, but to get the bounty on our heads!' Sam Baker growled.

'What they doing here?' Clooney asked again.

Black Bill lowered his head and started to laugh. 'Ain't it obvious, Jett?'

'Nope.'

'Them Texas Rangers are here to die.' Bodie went on laughing as his right hand hauled one of his .44s from its holster and cocked its hammer. 'I'll make damn sure of that!'

16

Sergeant Buck Macready had not forgiven himself for firing his gun and possibly alerting the outlaws of their presence in Satan's Pass. He had rested with his head against his saddle on the floor of the dry sandy valley for hours watching the moonlit ridge opposite him. Every instinct he had honed over the years seemed to warn him that trouble was headed in their direction. Macready knew that all the younger Texas Rangers had been sleeping since they had crawled into their bedrolls, but he could not close his own eyes.

Macready knew that he alone had to remain alert. Just in case his gut-feeling was correct.

He glanced across at Ethan Clark who lay on his side beside his horse. The major was either asleep or vainly trying to find rest like himself.

The Texas Ranger rubbed at his eyes and inhaled deeply. He was quite as tired as any of his comrades and yet sleep refused to come to him. He stared up at the high ridge again and then felt the hair on the back of his neck rise. Something had caught his attention but he could not work out what. His eyes narrowed as he focused through the moonlight.

Then he saw them.

The light of the bright moon danced off the metal of their Winchester rifles as the eight desperadoes made their way along the crest of the ridge and stealthily down into its crags.

Macready pulled his blanket off him and rolled away from his saddle and the resting horse. He continued rolling over and over until he reached the side of the slumbering major.

He shook Clark's shoulder hard.

'Wake up, Major! Wake up!' There was an urgency in his voice as he watched Clark's eyelids flicker.

Ethan Clark twisted and turned until

he freed himself of the rough blanket and then stared bleary-eyed into the face above his own.

'Buck? What's eating you?' the officer protested. 'Get back to sleep.'

'We got us company, sir! And they're loaded for bear.'

Clark rose up on an elbow. 'What you mean?'

Macready moved closer to his superior and pointed up at the high ridge opposite them. For a moment the major could not see anything. Then he noticed the flashing of moonlight on the outlaws as they moved into position.

'See them?'

'Yep, I see them, Buck.' Clark crawled out of his bedding and scrambled up on to his knees. His eyes focussed keenly on the figures who were moving above them. 'I count eight.'

'Check. That's exactly how many I've counted, sir.'

'That tallies with the information I was given about Black Bill Bodie and his gang, Buck.' Clark sighed. 'That must be them up there.'

'They're all carrying carbines, Major.'

'And we're their targets! C'mon, Buck. We have to warn the boys, and we ain't got much time.'

The two men tried to use the shadows to their advantage. They crawled as fast as they could across the still warm sand towards the rest of their sleeping platoon.

'Are you sure they're the darn *hombres* we've been sent here to ferret out, sir?' Macready asked.

'Reckon they must be,' said Clark. He placed a hand over the mouth of the first sleeping Texas Ranger, then woke him up. 'Easy, son. Get your rifle ready. We've got some uninvited visitors.'

One by one the two men woke all of their younger recruits, then rested beside their horses. They could see Black Bill and his men still moving across the rocks.

'Get your rifle ready, Buck,' ordered Clark, dragging his own carbine from its scabbard beneath the saddle. 'We've little time left by my figuring.'

'Maybe if we try and get saddled up, Major.' Macready panted as he tried to steady his nerves. 'If we can get mounted we might be able to ride out of the range of their rifles.'

'There's no time. No time,' Clark insisted. His eyes darted all over the eerie rockface before them. 'Just make sure your rifle's loaded. They're getting ready to open up on us.'

Buck Macready checked his weapon, then dragged a box of Winchester cartridges from his saddlebags.

'We're sitting ducks, Major.'

Ethan Clark nodded in agreement.

'You're dead right, Buck.'

'What we gonna do? When them varmints are in position over there they're gonna open up and pick us off one by one.'

The officer bit a chunk of tobacco off and chewed it thoughtfully. He had only one answer and no matter how he turned it around in his head, it still came out the same way.

'There's only one thing we can do, Buck. We have to use the horses as shields.'

Macready's jaw dropped.

'What? Did you just say we gotta use our horses as shields, Major?'

Clark offered the tobacco-block to his sergeant.

'Yep. That's what I said, Buck. Much as I hate the idea, the only things we've got to take cover behind are our mounts.'

Macready accepted the block, bit off a chunk and started to chew it slowly.

'Damn!' he muttered.

Clark patted the shoulder of the kneeling man. Then he moved quickly along the line of terrified Texas Rangers. He told each of them that they had to keep their mounts tied to the heavy saddles on the ground. They also had to keep the horses between themselves and the rocks opposite them. When he returned to the still-chewing Macready he manhandled his own horse away from the rockface behind them until it was standing directly in the line of fire.

Macready reluctantly did the same, then watched as their eighteen men all copied their actions.

'We'll never get out of here without a hoss under our backsides, sir.'

'We'll all be dead if them outlaws start shooting and we've nothing to hide behind, Buck. Either way our options are pretty limited.'

Buck Macready nodded. 'Damn! I know that you're right, but it still don't make it any less bad.'

Clark was about to reply when he heard the unmistakable sound of the outlaws' Winchesters being cocked and readied. It was a noise which chilled the souls of the Texas Rangers.

Both men spat at exactly the same time.

There were no more words. The high valley wall before them erupted with rifle fire. Vicious bullets blasted down from the eight repeating rifles that were trained on the Texas Rangers. Within a heartbeat nothing except deafening shots could be heard in Satan's Pass. Some horses were hit and made blood-curdling sounds of distress as the outlaws' bullets tore into their unprotected flesh. Echoes seemed to amplify the sound until every ear-drum felt as if it were ready to burst within the skulls of the trapped law officers.

The Texas Rangers' horses continued to take the full impact of the outlaws' never-ending rifle volleys. Blood and flesh cascaded over the crouching men. One by one the animals fell as their large bodies were riddled by the cruel bullets.

'Return fire!' Major Clark yelled out at the top of his voice. 'Start shooting, men!'

The terrified Texas Rangers started to fire their own rifles up at their enemies. Yet the night air was now filled with almost impenetrable gunsmoke. Its acrid stench filled their nostrils as they blasted back. None of the Rangers could see their targets as the smoke grew more and more dense. All they could see was the white-hot flashes of rifle barrels spewing lead as the outlaws continued to fire their trusty Winchesters.

'Keep shooting, boys!' Macready urged the confused platoon. 'Keep aiming at the white flashes.'

Clark's right arm was aching as he pushed the mechanism of his own Winchester up and down between shots. Sweat poured down his face as red tapers burned past him and ricocheted off the rockface behind him. A thousand screaming thoughts filled his mind. Were the outlaws moving as they fired? Were they working their way closer to him and his trapped men? Had his platoon been sent on a suicidal mission for some reason that he might never learn?

'This ain't good, sir,' shouted Macready.

The major was about to reply when he saw Buck Macready forced backwards into the hard rockface. There was a hole in the centre of his chest as big as a fist. Blood ran from his mouth as he managed to turn his head and look at his commanding officer. Then a blank expression overwhelmed Macready's face. The Ranger fell forward lifelessly.

'Buck!' Clark called out in a vain attempt to raise his voice above the deafening noise.

For a split second every one of the younger troopers turned and looked at the body beside the major. Clark gritted his teeth and screamed at them.

'Keep firing! It's your only chance. Get closer to your horses.'

Before the words had left his dry lips, he watched in horror as three more of his men were torn to shreds by the outlaws' deadly bullets.

Then the Texas Rangers' commanding officer was hit off his knees by the impact of a rifle bullet as it cut through him. He lay on his side for a few seconds and watched as blood poured from the ugly wound in his tunic. The pain came a few moments later.

A thousand branding-irons could not have inflicted more pain on the downed Clark. He screwed his eyes up and forced himself up off the sand. The outlaws' shots were becoming even more accurate as the long rifles found their range. Lumps of horseflesh were flying in all directions as Clark watched more of his platoon of youngsters falling under the ceaseless outlaw volley.

Pitiful cries rang out into the night air as the major tried to give what was left of them encouragement.

'K . . . keep firing, men.' Clark's voice faded until there was nothing left but uncontrolled coughing. Blood dripped from his mouth with every beat of his pounding heart.

He knew that every passing second meant more and more of his blood was being pumped out of the horrific bullet hole.

The severely wounded Ethan Clark moved closer to his fallen horse which lay in front of him. His hands were slippery from the gore but he managed to cock the mechanism of his Winchester once more. He rested its long barrel on the animal's shoulder. He pushed himself as close to the animal as was possible until he was pressed up against its blood-soaked back.

His mind began to fill with a strange fog that he could not shake off. It felt as if his mind had fallen into a whirlpool which he could neither understand or stop from dragging him down into its bottomless depths.

Blood trickled from his mouth as he desperately tried to concentrate on the fleeting glimpses of outlaws opposite on the moonlit rockface. He steadied the Winchester and inhaled.

Clark squeezed the trigger and fired. The rifle kick made it drop from his hands. He slid back on to the sand and stared at it. He heard the unmistakable cry of an outlaw being hit by his bullet echo above the deafening sounds of bullets.

For the first time in twenty years, he started to pray.

17

They had covered a lot of ground across the top of the ridge on their quest to reach Devil's Peak unnoticed by Black Bill Bodie's outlaw gang. Yet the sound of the battle that raged in Satan's Pass had slowed their progress over the previous few minutes. The Valko Kid pulled his reins up to his chest and stopped the large white stallion. Clem Everett drew level with him and halted his own mount.

'Who on earth is making all that ruckus, Kid?' gasped the US marshal, as they both listened to the echoing noise of ceaseless gunshots drifting on the cool night air. 'Sounds like someone started a war someplace.'

Valko bit his lips and raised himself until he was balancing in his stirrups.

'Whoever they are, they sound serious, Clem.'

Everett rubbed his face. 'But who could be fighting all the way up here, in the middle of nowhere?'

The Kid did not reply at first. He carefully studied the ridge that their horses were standing upon. He was trying to find a safe trail that led down from their precarious perch, which would lead them towards the rifle shots.

'Maybe the Governor sent somebody else after Black Bill, Clem. I reckon that Bodie and his cohorts didn't take kindly to being visited.'

The marshal pointed at the distant flashes of light which were coming out from Satan's Pass.

'That must be where the shooting is, Valko.'

'That's Satan's Pass, Clem.' The Kid sighed. He knew that was one place where the odds were not even. 'That's the trail we were meant to be taking to get to Devil's Peak.'

Everett grunted.

'Do you reckon that some innocent folks might have been heading through the valley and Bodie and his men mistook them for us?'

Valko ran a hand along the neck of his horse.

'You could be right. It sure sounds like a bushwhacking to me.'

Clem Everett rested both his wrists on his saddle horn.

'Just like you warned me, Kid. You said that they'd try and bushwhack us there. Maybe they think that them poor critters are us loaded down with the ransom money.'

'Could be, Clem.' Valko eased his mount forward a few steps and then saw where they might be able to steer their horses off the high ridge and down toward the noisy battle. 'There's only one way to find out, though.'

'You ain't thinking of heading over there are you, son?'

'I sure am. You game to follow me, Clem?'

The lawman looked to where the Kid was indicating.

'You figuring on trying to ride down

that slope? It don't look like any horse could negotiate that slope without breaking its neck or the rider on its back.'

Valko nodded.

'Can you just ignore that without even trying to help?'

Everett was nervous. Even in daylight it would have looked like a dangerous route. At night with only the moon to guide them, it seemed virtually impossible.

'Are you sure that our horses can make it down there? It's as steep as a cliff.'

The Kid carefully turned his magnificent mount and urged it towards the edge of the ridge. Sand was shifting beneath the weight of the stallion.

'I'm going to try it, Clem. Follow me down if you've the nerve.'

The lawman watched as the Valko Kid leaned back in his saddle and allowed Snow to descend the slope. He sighed heavily, then tapped his spurs and forced his gelding over the lip of the ridge and down after his young friend's mount.

* * *

It seemed as if they had been riding for ever across the arid landscape, yet neither horsemen would falter from the chosen course. They were headed to Satan's Pass because they knew that the men they sought had to be there. There were also others that might require help.

Nothing could stop them.

Both riders had noticed that the shooting had stopped only a few minutes after they had set out across the distance between the high ridge and the deep valley, yet they had continued.

The horrific sight which greeted them as they rode into Satan's Pass caused both Valko and Everett to rein in.

The Kid dismounted first. He silently handed his reins up to the older rider, then inhaled deeply. Valko had witnessed many sickening sights in his time but nothing that had prepared him for this.

Every one of the Texas Rangers' horses was dead. Their large bodies still oozed blood and guts from the numerous bullet holes that had perforated their hides.

Cautiously, the Valko Kid walked across the blood-soaked sand and rested his hands on his gun grips. He averted his eyes from the bodies of Major Clark and his men, which littered the ground behind the dead horses. The bodies were just a mass of crimson pulp. Valko shivered and then looked up and noticed the three bodies of outlaws hanging from the rocks above them.

'At least they managed to kill a few of the bushwhackers.'

Clem Everett dismounted and moved towards the brooding Kid. When he too saw the state of the dead Texas Rangers, he turned away.

'We're too late, son.' Everett sighed.

'We could have prevented this killing if we'd been able to make better time.'

Valko looked into his friend's eyes.

'This weren't a killing, Clem. This was a massacre,' he corrected.

Before the US marshal could say anything, the younger man threw himself back on to his saddle and gathered up his reins. Valko steadied Snow and stared through the moonlight at the lawman.

'You coming, Clem?'

Everett grabbed his saddle horn and pulled himself on top of his gelding.

'Where?'

'Devil's Peak!' Valko snapped angrily. 'I reckon it's time someone stopped Black Bill Bodie.'

'Remember, Kid,' the marshal warned, 'Bodie is fast.'

'He'll have to be, Clem.'

Both horses thundered away from their masters' gruesome discovery and headed at full gallop for the distant mesa.

18

The small crude hideout was at the base of the massive rock known as Devil's Peak. The five remaining outlaws had returned to its remote safety after destroying the platoon. Black Bill Bodie had taken his fury at not finding a single golden coin of the $100,000 ransom in the saddlebags of the Texas Rangers out on their dead bodies. The bloodstained rifle stocks of both his Winchesters bore grim testament to his earlier anger.

'We lost Jake, Treat and Joey back there, Bill,' Frank Grange noted with a raised eyebrow.

'Who gives a damn?' Bodie said surlily.

'What were them Texas Rangers heading here for if they hadn't been bringing the gold, Bill?' Jett Clooney asked his snorting gang-leader. 'It don't make no sense at all. They never come here into this neck of the woods.'

Bodie glanced around his four remaining men and spat at the ground. 'Where's my gold? I was meant to have the ransom by now.'

Sitting on a boulder near Bodie, one-eyed Sam Baker nursed his left leg and the neat bullet hole that had gone right through its calf muscle.

'I thought you said that Clem Everett was bringing the loot with Valko, Bill?'

Bodie nodded. 'Yeah, that's what I thought was happening, Sam. But we ain't seen hide nor hair of them varmints, have we?'

'You sure that your important pal in Austin is telling you the truth?' asked Frank Grange. 'He ain't trying to trick you, is he?'

'He wouldn't dare!' Black Bill rose to his full height and spat at the ground again. He thought about the question for a while and then looked around at his remaining men.

'He might,' Baker added. 'Not many

of them city dudes know about you.'

'But I got this important chunk of paper here,' Black Bill said, tapping his shirt and the document which rested close to his skin. 'It's valuable.'

Grange looked up at Bodie.

'Are ya sure? We only got that bastard's word for it, Bill.'

Bodie's expression altered. He had not questioned the fact that he and his gang had been hired to steal the document or that it was worth a small fortune to whoever owned it. That was the information which had been given to him. Until now, he'd had no reason to doubt its accuracy.

Black Bill reached inside his shirt, pulled the document out and stared at it thoughtfully.

'It looks important enough, don't it?' he asked.

His four men all nodded. None of them was willing to upset Bodie any further.

'Looks darn important to me, Bill,' Clooney said, loudly.

Bodie's eyes flashed around his seated men. He knew that only Grange had ever spoken the truth to him over the years. The buck-toothed outlaw was too stupid to lie or fear anything his leader might inflict upon him. Black Bill moved closer to Grange and held the folded document under his nose.

'Do ya honestly think that it's worth a hundred thousand dollars in gold coin, Frank? Well?'

Grange shrugged. 'How would I know? I can't even read. What's all them words on it?'

Bodie turned until the moon was at his back and stared at the strange writing.

'It ain't English. Could be Mexican.'

Jett Clooney lit a cigarette and inhaled deeply, then put his tobacco pouch back inside his vest pocket.

'I reckon that it must be valuable if it's written in some foreign tongue, Bill. Nothing written in English is ever worth nothing.'

Black Bill nodded in agreement.

'Yeah. That makes sense. I reckon it must be some kinda treaty or the like. Maybe it's the deeds to Texas.'

The outlaws all laughed.

'We might own Texas and not even know it, Bill,' Baker piped up as he nursed his throbbing leg. 'Damn. This hurts real bad. I reckon I need me some doctorin'.'

'Hush the hell up, Sam,' said Bodie. He slid the document back inside his filthy shirt and walked away from them. 'You can't walk proper, anyway. That hole in ya leg won't make any damn difference.'

'It might go bad,' Baker protested. 'I could end up losing my foot or leg.'

'You already lost an eye. You ought to be used to losing parts of ya worthless hide by now, Sam,' Bodie grunted as he stared out along Satan's Pass.

Frank Grange jumped to his feet and ran to Black Bill's side.

'What's wrong, Bill?' he asked. 'You seen something?'

Black Bill raised a hand until the

outlaw's mouth was silenced.

'Hush up, Frank. Listen. Do ya hear that?'

Grange strained and put both hands to his ears.

'Hear what?'

Bodie spat at the ground again.

'Riders, Frank. I hear riders.'

'Are you sure?' Grange asked.

Black Bill Bodie pointed into the moonlit valley and the trace of dust that hung in the star-filled sky.

'Yep. We got us company coming,' Bodie announced. 'Get ya guns and rifles loaded boys. I think Everett and Valko have gotten here at last.'

* * *

The Valko Kid hung over the neck of his powerful mount and allowed the stallion to eat up the sandy ground with its hoofs. Clem Everett tried desperately not to lose sight of his young companion.

Then the Kid leaned back and

hauled his reins up to his chin with his clenched fists. The big white horse stopped within yards of its master's command. Thick dust drifted up into the moonlit air around him. The Kid stood in his stirrups and stared ahead into the murky distance like an eagle locating its prey. Everett stopped his horse next to his silent companion and tried to get his breath back.

'W . . . what you seen?'

'You gonna wheeze that loud when the shooting starts, Clem?' Valko asked, lowering himself back down on to his saddle.

'What you see, Kid?'

'I ain't too sure. Reckon it must be Black Bill and the vermin he rides with.' Valko's voice had a coldness to it that the marshal had not heard before.

Everett kept his horse in check as his tired eyes tried to make out what the Kid was staring at.

'I can just about see Devil's Peak, son,' he admitted. 'If you say that you think the outlaws are there, I'll have to take your word for it.'

'They're there, Clem!' the Kid said firmly. 'Believe me, they're there.'

'What we gonna do?' The lawman had no stomach for riding blindly into the rifle barrels of such deadly opponents. 'If they're waiting at the end of the valley, we can't go any further.'

'You're right. We can't ride any closer or we'll be in range of their Winchesters.' Valko dismounted quickly and wrapped his reins around his saddle horn. 'We've seen what they can do with their rifles, Clem.'

The marshal eased himself off his horse and held on to his reins tightly as he moved closer to his friend's side. He then noticed that the Kid was studying the rockfaces on either side of them.

'What you thinking about, son?'

'I'm thinking that we ought to try and climb up there and make our way across the top of the ridge before they get the notion to ride over the top of it and bushwhack us the same way they did to those poor Texas Rangers.'

The lawman leaned back and stared up at the rugged wall of rock to their right.

'That'll be a darn hard climb, Valko. I ain't sure that I could make it all the way up there.'

The Kid nodded.

'Yep. It is kinda high. And we've only got an hour to get up there and move along towards Devil's Rock.'

'Why an hour?'

The Kid pulled his Winchester out of its scabbard.

'Because that's about all the time we have until the sun comes up.'

Everett dragged his own repeating rifle out from under his saddle and cranked its mechanism.

'I hadn't thought of that. We don't wanna get caught half-way up that chunk of rock when the sun rises.'

'It'll be a close-run thing, Clem,' Valko said, looking at the sky knowingly. 'C'mon!'

The Valko Kid walked to the foot of

the high rockface and looked up. As the lawman reached his side he stared into the trusting face.

'After you, son.' Everett gestured.

'Are you sure that you can make it, Clem?'

The question went unanswered. Both men could feel the ground beneath them tremble.

'What's happening?'

The Valko Kid swung around on his heels and cocked the Winchester in his hands. He held it at hip-level and screwed up his eyes. He stared along the valley into the eerie blue moonlight.

'They're coming!'

19

The bullets tore through Satan's Pass from the weapons of the five riders as they bore down on the two men. Everett cranked his repeating rifle, lifted it to his shoulder and fired into the murky haze before him. The Valko Kid felt the heat of the outlaws' bullets as they burned through the night air.

'They're getting closer, Kid!' Everett shouted. He fired again. 'Ain't you gonna shoot?'

Valko saw the charging horsemen bearing down on the marshal and himself. He could not make out whether Bodie was leading his men or trailing them as their guns and rifles continued to blast their deadly lead towards them.

He began to fire the Winchester furiously but this was not his favoured weapon. He had never mastered the rifle in the same way as he had his prized Colts. Valko watched in horror as he saw one of the horses fall heavily and send its rider hurtling over its neck.

The Kid continued firing as the remaining riders spurred their horses on. Bullets tore up the ground at his feet, driving him towards the rockface. Then a rifle bullet ricocheted off the rocks beside him, sending blinding dust into his eyes.

Valko felt the carbine being torn from his grip as another outlaw bullet hit the barrel. It fell from his hands as he buckled and covered his eyes.

Ignoring a volley of red-hot tapers ripping across the moonlit valley, Everett ran to Valko's side and shielded the younger man with his own body. The marshal kept firing and watched as he managed to take Jett Clooney off his saddle with a deadly accurate shot.

'You OK, Kid?' the lawman shouted above the noise of the bullets. Their spine chilling echoes resounded around Satan's Pass. 'Are you hit?'

'I ain't hit,' Valko replied. He wiped the dust from his eyes with the tails of his bandanna. 'Keep shooting, Clem. I'll be OK as soon as I can see.'

One shot after another left the barrel of the Winchester as Everett blasted at the outlaws. He could see that the three riders had stopped advancing. With their rifles empty they were now fanning the hammers of their handguns.

Valko grabbed his rifle off the ground and handed it to the marshal just as Everett's own Winchester became empty of cartridges.

'Good timing, Kid!' Everett said.

The Kid dragged the lawman down on to his knees.

'Keep low, Clem. They're too good with them guns of theirs to give them a big target.'

Valko dragged both his Colts from their holsters and started to fire.

'They're too far away!' the Kid exclaimed. 'Out of range for six-shooters.'

Everett cocked the Kid's Winchester and fired. His bullet hit Sam Baker high. The US marshal watched as the one-eyed outlaw crashed from his saddle into the sand.

'Not out of range for a Winchester though, Kid,' Everett said.

Only Black Bill Bodie and Frank Grange remained in their saddles. They had made a mistake in attacking two men who were capable of fighting back and they knew it. They'd emptied their rifles and the two men were still alive. Bodie knew that the range of his Remington .44s required him to get closer. He was unwilling to do so.

'One of them bastards still has a rifle, Frankie.' Bodie spat. 'And he knows how to use the darn thing.'

'What we gonna do, Bill?' Grange asked as his horse reared up and kicked at the gunsmoke-filled air. 'We've run out of cannon-fodder.'

'Let's get back to the hideout, Frankie.' Bodie turned the pinto stallion and spurred hard. The animal responded and galloped away.

The hapless Frank Grange steadied his skittish mount and turned its head away from the two men who had fought back. As he sank his spurs into the animal's sides, he felt something hit his back. When his chest exploded, he realized that it had been another well-placed bullet from the Winchester in Clem Everett's hands. The horse bolted as Grange slid sideways off his saddle.

With a lifeless body beneath its hoofs, the terrified mount dragged what was left of Frank Grange for more than a hundred yards before the outlaw's boot finally freed itself from the stirrup. Grange's lifeless carcass rolled over a dozen times before coming to a rest against a wall of rock.

Clem Everett jumped back to his feet.

'Did you see that shot, Kid?'

The Valko Kid did not reply. He holstered his guns and then ran across the sand and leapt over the tail of his white stallion. He landed in his saddle, rammed his boots in his stirrups and galloped after Black Bill Bodie.

Everett lowered the rifle and watched in awe.

20

There seemed to be no escape. It was a desperate Black Bill Bodie who whipped his reins ferociously across the shoulders of his large pinto as he headed toward his hideout at the foot of Devil's Peak. He could hear the rider behind him gaining with every pounding of his heart. Bodie stood in his stirrups and looked over his shoulder through the dust that was being kicked up off the hoofs of his galloping mount.

Then he saw the rider behind him.

Black Bill could not imagine how the white horse was capable of cutting down the distance between them so easily. He whipped his pinto harder and harder in a vain effort to outride the powerful animal behind him.

He had heard many stories about the famed Valko Kid. He'd never taken any of them seriously. The sight of the powerful white stallion suddenly made him wonder if the tales might not have been true after all.

Bodie dragged one of his .44s from its holster and held his arm out behind him. He fired over and over again at his relentless pursuer, but Valko kept on chasing him.

Bodie wondered whether it might not be wiser to avoid his camp and find a better place to try and fend off his hunter. The merciless outlaw realized that once he dismounted, and the shooting started, his pinto stallion would probably run off leaving him to try and escape this devilish place on foot.

Even Satan would find that impossible.

The ruthless outlaw had almost reached his hideout at the foot of the great mesa when he dragged his reins to the left and spurred hard. The pinto did not miss a step and carried on into a long, winding canyon.

Dust rose into the dry air off the

hoofs of the fleeing rider as Bodie forced his huge stallion to find more and more speed. The stars above faded as the sky started to show the first signs that a new day was imminent.

Yet neither horseman noticed. They had other, more deadly things on their minds.

Both knew that it was now only a matter of time before one of them died. Neither wanted it to be him.

The Valko Kid gripped his reins in his hands and allowed Snow to find his own incredible pace. As always, the horse did not fail him. Defying his years, Snow thundered on.

Stride after stride, the powerful white stallion gained on the pinto. The Kid stood in his stirrups and leaned over the horse's neck as Bodie's bullets tried to stop his relentless pursuit.

Valko pulled one of his guns from its holster and cocked its hammer. Whatever it said on his wanted posters, the Kid could not shoot anyone in the back. He balanced in his stirrups and trained the Colt on the man ahead of him, waiting for one chance to stop Bodie.

Valko knew that he had to prevent Black Bill Bodie from continuing his reign of terror somehow. If he did not, countless more innocent people would be killed by the unholy outlaw.

Then the Kid's blue eyes saw the pinto stallion being hauled to its left and forced up a rocky rise in an attempt to get to higher ground. With unimaginable accuracy, Valko fired three shots a few feet ahead of the pinto's nose, into the slope. A cloud of dust billowed up into the eyes of the large horse, stopping it in its tracks. Bodie went over the shoulder of his mount and crashed into the ground.

The Kid shouted into the ear of his faithful horse:

'C'mon, Snow. We got the critter!'

The white stallion ate up the distance between the fallen outlaw and himself. Valko pulled back on his reins just as he saw the glint of one of Bodie's

Remingtons as it was raised.

The white flash was blinding.

The Kid felt the heat of the bullet pass his face and tear his black Stetson off his head. Its deafening sound filled the canyon.

Before Valko knew what was happening he felt himself hit the ground heavily. For a few eternal seconds the Kid lay on his back. Then he heard something which shook the fog out of his head.

The white stallion charged at the dazed Bodie and knocked the outlaw off his feet.

With the same courage as his master, Snow had bought his master a few precious seconds.

Valko did not waste one of them. He jumped back to his feet and blinked hard. He felt a small trace of blood trickle down from the graze on his hairline. He wiped it away with the back of his left hand.

Black Bill got back to his feet and snarled at the Kid.

It was a blood-chilling sight, even to the likes of Valko. His mind raced as he wondered how many other people had faced this gruesome vision just before being killed.

Valko's right hand touched the empty holster on his right hip. Then he noticed his Colt .45 on the ground more than twenty feet from where he stood.

His left thumb flicked the leather safety loop off the hammer of the gun in his left holster. He swallowed hard when he noticed that Bodie still had both his Remingtons. One was holstered and the other was gripped firmly in his right hand against his thigh.

'So we meet at last, Valko,' Black Bill shouted as he staggered away from his horse.

'Looks that way, Black Bill,' replied the Kid, flexing the fingers of his left hand.

'Now we'll find out who really is the fastest gun alive,' Bodie snarled. 'I figure you'll be darn upset in a couple of minutes' time.'

Valko started to walk sideways and closer to his gun, which lay on the ground. He never once took his eyes from the devilish figure before him. The Kid had learned long ago that even to blink was to die.

'You talk big, but you've got one of your hoglegs in your hand, Black Bill. I ain't even got both my guns in their holsters.'

Bodie stopped moving and raised the weapon in his hand until it was aimed at the Kid.

'You reckon that it makes a difference, Valko?'

Valko lowered his head.

'It might. Guess I'll never know, will I?'

Bodie's thumb cocked the hammer.

'Nope!'

Using his natural agility, Valko twisted and leapt sideways just as his left hand drew the Colt from its hand-tooled holster. His thumb hauled the hammer back a fraction of a second before he squeezed its trigger.

Bodie's bullet left the barrel of the Remington at exactly the same time that Valko's .45 fired.

As the Kid landed, he plucked his other gun off the ground with his right hand. He cocked and fired it before he rolled over.

Valko steadied himself on his knees, and watched Bodie stagger backwards until he regained his balance. Valko cocked the hammers of both his guns again and rose cautiously to his feet.

Black Bill Bodie spat at the ground between them. He then looked down at the two well-placed bullet holes in the centre of his large chest. Both had managed to avoid the crossed ammunition belts he wore like gruesome jewellery.

'Damn. You killed me, you bastard,' Bodie growled in disbelief. 'You up and killed Black Bill.'

The sound of Clem Everett's approaching gelding drew Bodie's attention. He swayed and raised his Remington and aimed it at the lawman.

Valko gritted his teeth and then fired both his Colts again.

He watched as Bodie was lifted off his feet and crashed lifelessly in a bloody heap beside the legs of his pinto.

'Now I've killed you, Black Bill!'

Before Everett had reached the horrific scene, Valko had already mounted the white stallion.

'You got him, Kid!' the marshal panted.

The Kid handed the document he had taken from Bodie's body to the weary lawman.

'Whatever this paper is, it cost a lot of lives, Clem.'

'But you killed him, Kid. You were the fastest.'

'There's always someone faster, Clem,' Valko muttered. 'I just ain't met him yet.'

Everett lowered his head and sighed. He watched as the white stallion slowly walked away with its master slumped in his saddle.

'Where you going, Kid?'

Valko looked over his broad shoulder.

'Back to Satan's Pass. I got me a lot of men to bury before the vultures wake up.'

Clem Everett spurred his gelding and silently trailed the younger rider back along the moonlit canyon. It would take two men to lay so many to rest, he thought.

21

It was the morning of the twentieth. Clem Everett had arrived in Austin the previous night. He had waited outside the Governor's mansion until morning light had brought the array of official buildings to life once more. He had noticed that his trail clothes had not brought the same condescending attention as his Sunday best. Perhaps it was the dried blood that stained the sleeves of his tattered jacket and sun-bleached boots which caused the people in top hats to avoid him as if he had the plague.

It might have been the look that was etched into his haggard features. The look of a man who had been to hell and back and somehow survived.

When the mansion's highly polished doors eventually opened, the marshal rose to his feet from the bench directly opposite the marble building and headed straight for them.

The officials who were meant to guard the Governor's mansion somehow recognized Everett from his previous visit and ushered him through the cool corridors until once again he reached the office where he had first met Hyram Sloane.

He knew every inch of the marble waiting-area. He had stared at its stone patterns for a long time on his first visit.

This time the battered and bruised marshal would be forced to wait even longer for an audience. Clem Everett rested on a hard bench with his dust-and-sweat-caked Stetson in his hands. When the large clock at the end of the corridor chimed for the third time Everett finally lost his patience. It was ten.

The seasoned lawman stood and walked to the familiar door and opened it. He entered the secretary's office and looked around at its luxurious decoration. A declaration of wealth which was only bettered by Sloane's own office.

Everett strode across the highly polished floor towards the door that he knew led to the Governor's office. A few strides away from the large door the marshal paused and noticed that Sloane's name had been removed from it.

He hesitated.

Everett looked around him again. This was definitely the right place, he concluded. He had not mistaken one of the many identical doors leading off the reception area. This was the office of Jacob Francis.

The marshal took one more step and then was halted by a powerful voice behind him. He turned and looked at the well-rounded military officer.

'Who are you, sir?' General Jackson asked as he walked towards Everett. 'Why are you here?'

'I've come to see the Governor.'

The general dropped his eyes for a brief moment, then he looked back up again into the eyes of the weary lawman.

'You must be Marshal Everett, I take it.'

Everett nodded. 'Yep. How come you know me?'

'Come with me, Marshal.' Jackson walked around the lawman and opened the door to Sloane's office. 'Take a seat.'

Everett heard the door close behind him as he sat down in the same chair that he had used on his previous visit. Jackson walked around the desk and sat down opposite him.

'My name is General Tiberius Jackson, Marshal.'

Everett leaned forward in his chair.

'What's all this about, General? I've come to deliver something to Governor Sloane. If you can tell him I'm here . . . '

'That would be rather tricky, Marshal,' said Jackson. He tapped his fingertips together. 'Hyram Sloane is dead.'

Everett's expression changed.

'Dead?'

Jackson raised both his eyebrows and nodded.

'Yes.'

'How?' the lawman asked curiously.

'Suicide.'

The word burned into Everett.

'Are you telling me that he killed himself? Why would he do that?'

'Shame? Guilt? Who can understand the motives of a disturbed mind, Marshal? Certainly not I.' Jackson sat upright in his chair and toyed with the pipes in the wooden rack next to the ink blotter. Everett knew that there had been no pipes or a rack there on his last visit.

'I don't understand. He told me to try and bring this document to him before noon on the twentieth.' Everett patted his breast pocket. 'It's only just a little after ten. I made it here with time to spare.'

Jackson gripped the stem of one of his pipes between his teeth and held out a hand.

'May I see the document?'

Reluctantly, Everett reached inside his jacket and pulled out the folded document. He handed it over to the military commander.

'When did the Governor kill himself, General Jackson?'

Jackson studied the document carefully. Then he opened a drawer at his right and slid the document into it. He locked the drawer and put the key in his vest pocket. Jackson then looked up into Everett's confused face.

'Texas owes you its gratitude, Marshal Everett.'

'When did Sloane kill himself?' The marshal repeated his question.

'On the evening of the sixteenth.' Jackson pointed the stem of his pipe at the plastered ceiling above their heads. 'In his bedroom.'

Everett rubbed his whiskered chin.

'Something smells around here, sir. Are you trying to tell me that Hyram Sloane suddenly lost his mind and decided to kill himself before he even knew whether I had succeeded in retrieving the document?'

General Jackson nodded. A hint of a smile played on his lips.

'I do not care if you believe me or not, Marshal. Our business is over. You may leave now.'

Clem Everett inhaled deeply. There was a wagonload of questions inside him that he could not fathom. He knew that something was not right and yet his mind was not corrupt enough to work out exactly what.

'Our business ain't over, Jackson,' he snapped.

The general struck a match, held its flame above his pipe-bowl and puffed.

'I will excuse your tone because you are tired, Marshal. But I see nothing else for us to discuss.'

'Governor Sloane promised me that he would have a pardon for the Valko Kid awaiting my return. Without the help of the Kid I could never have gotten that document back here.'

The words washed over the emotionless Jackson.

'I know nothing of this Valko Kid or a pardon.'

Clem Everett rose abruptly and slammed his fist on top of the desk.

'Get that pardon, General. Valko earned it and I'm damned if I'm gonna ride back and tell him that some overweight army dude couldn't be bothered to look for it. If you can't find the original, then have a new one written up.'

Jackson puffed slowly.

'I am in temporary control of this office, Marshal. I do not have the legal powers to do what you ask. But even if I could, I would not do anything to help a filthy outlaw.'

Everett walked to the window and stared out at the trimly kept gardens. His weary brain could not understand what exactly was happening.

'So the Valko Kid is still a wanted outlaw?'

Jackson nodded silently.

The US marshal walked back to the desk. His eyes narrowed and he stared down at the man seated in the governor's chair.

'What kinda animal are you, Jackson?'

'A political one, Marshal Everett. You would never understand.'

'I've met some vermin in my time but nothing that compares to you, Jackson.'

The general laughed.

'Get out before I have you thrown out or even locked up. We frown on violent behaviour in Austin. Go back to the ranges if you wish to throw your weight around. You might be a big man there but here you are nothing. Nothing!'

Everett shook his head in a mixture of disgust and total confusion. He wanted to beat the arrogance out of the general but knew that if he did, he might never see the light of day again.

'If you ever set foot out there in the real world, I'll beat you to within an inch of your life, Jackson,' the marshal warned.

'And if you ever return here, I'll have

you executed by firing-squad,' the general countered.

Everett stormed out of the office. His high-heeled boots echoed around the rooms and corridors of the mansion as he headed for fresh air.

General Jackson heard a rapping on a side door to his left.

'Come in, Jacob. He's gone.'

The door opened and Jacob Francis entered the governor's office with a twisted smile on his thin, pale features.

'I was listening, General. You were very good.'

Jackson puffed on his pipe and nodded in agreement as the thin figure reached the desk.

'I think all the loose ends are neatly tied up, Jacob. That was the final pink ribbon.'

Francis leaned over the desk.

'You played it brilliantly. The entire thing has been resolved exactly as we planned. I was expecting Everett to cause us problems but he was no match for you.'

'He was putty in my hands, Jacob.'

'You frightened him. You actually frightened him.'

Jackson stood and walked to the large bookcase in a corner of the room and pressed a hidden button on the third shelf. A line of six mock books flicked open to reveal a cast-iron safe buried in the wall. He turned the dial back and forth until a loud click was heard. Jackson turned the handle down and opened its door. He pulled out two heavy bags and handed one to the eager Francis.

'Your share of the ransom money, Jacob.'

Both men beamed.

'It was simply too easy. Too damn easy.' Jackson laughed as he carried his bag to the desk and pulled a black leather satchel from out of one of its large lower drawers. He dropped the bag into it and relished the sound that the coins made. 'You are a genius, Jacob. A solid-gold genius.'

'To think that Hyram Sloane would

have used government gold to pay the ransom.' Francis grinned knowingly. 'No wonder he took his own life.'

'You are an artist, my friend. Even I could not tell the difference in the handwriting you forged and the genuine article,' the general admitted.

Jacob Francis knew that he had earned the praise that the military man heaped upon him. It had been he who had conspired with Sloane's political enemies and come up with the idea of having the valuable document stolen when it was in transit. He had used the governor's trust against him. With the help of Jackson's many spies, he had managed to find Black Bill Bodie, persuade him to steal the document and send a ransom letter demanding $100,000.

Sloane's political foes were waiting to shame the governor when the Texas parliament reconvened. Yet it had been General Tiberius Jackson who had added the final fatal chapter to the sordid tale. He had sent his highly paid assassins to the governor's private quarters a few days earlier. They had done what he had ordered: killed Hyram Sloane and made it appear as if the man had taken his own life. The deadly killers had obeyed their lethal instructions to the letter and left the carefully forged suicide note that Francis had provided next to the body with a single bullet in its skull.

'That was a very profitable exercise in imaginative politics, General,' Francis gloated as he looked inside the bag of golden coins in his hands.

Tiberius Jackson closed his black leather satchel and locked it.

'Indeed, and one that I think we might repeat when the elections are over, Jacob.'

Finale

US marshal Clem Everett sat at his desk inside his large office watching as Waco's citizens continually passed its open doorway. The lights were all lit and the coal-oil burned in their glass cases atop the tall poles to either side of the town's main street. He struck a match, touched the wick of his table-lamp and adjusted its flame. He set its glass funnel in place and rested his head in his hands for a few seconds until his tired eyes got used to the light.

Everett sighed heavily. Then he sat upright in his chair and picked up the single-sheet newspaper for the umpteenth time. He had tried to read it for hours and yet found it hard to get past the title banner:

THE WACO HERALD.
Tuesday 24 May.

He slumped down and rested his head on his folded arms on top of the desk. There had been a sick feeling gnawing at his innards since he had arrived back from Austin the previous day. He had been used by the system he was paid to uphold. Treated as a pawn in someone else's pitiful game of political machination. It had left a bitter taste in his mouth: a taste that no amount of whiskey had been able to wash away.

And yet the lawman did not feel angry for himself. He just felt that he had betrayed a young man whom he respected. The Valko Kid had not done anything except risk his own life once again to assist him.

Everett stared at the lamplight flickering the shadow of the whiskey bottle on his ink blotter. He had consumed half the bottle's contents since sitting down earlier that afternoon and yet it had failed to numb the pain.

Failed to rid his mind of the bitter truth that had mocked him like the words which had dripped like acid from the lips of General Tiberis Jackson four days earlier in the Governor's mansion.

He knew that he should have set out for Dry Gulch to tell Valko that they had both been tricked. That the young man was still wanted dead or alive. And yet he was ashamed to face the honest young man with such a declaration.

Then, as his tired eyes stared at the whiskey-bottle, he saw a familiar image reflected in its clear glass.

There was no mistaking the magnificent white stallion and its master, who was dressed entirely in black except for the long yellow bandanna that hung from his neck.

Marshal Everett sat up and looked at the Valko Kid astride his tall horse. There were mixed emotions coursing through his veins.

He was pleased to see Valko but also racked by guilt.

As he was about to rise to his feet he saw the young man dismount and loop his reins over the hitching pole directly outside the office door. Everett felt his heart pounding as the Kid stepped up on the boardwalk and entered.

'You look a tad troubled, Clem,' said the Kid. He rested his hip on the edge of the desk and lifted the bottle off the blotter. He sniffed at its neck, then set it down again with a knowing expression on his handsome features. 'Bad brew?'

Everett rested his spine against the hard chair-back. He looked at the face of his friend, then averted his eyes.

'I got bad news, Kid,' he muttered.

The Valko Kid reached across the desk and pulled the marshal's chin up until their eyes met.

'I figured that already, Clem.'

The lawman cleared his throat and raised his eyebrows.

'You did?'

'Yep. I had me a feeling that things didn't pan out the way you intended them to.'

Clem Everett stood, walked around the desk and looked hard at the thoughtful young man. No amount of whiskey could have prevented him from seeing the pain in the blue eyes of his pal.

'You know that we got tricked by them bastards in Austin?'

Valko nodded. 'I figured as much.'

'How? I only know the truth because I went there with that damn document. They said that Governor Sloane killed himself due to pressure of work or something. I figure he was killed by his political enemies. The varmints who are now running the show reckoned they knew nothing about your pardon for helping to recover the document. That means that you are still wanted.'

'Dead or alive.' The Kid finished the sentence.

Everett placed a hand on his friend's arm and shook his head sadly.

'I'm so sorry, Kid. I'd cut my right hand off if it would get you that pardon. But how did you figure out that something was wrong?'

Valko sighed.

'The hard way.'

‘Will you be going back to your little ranch in Dry Gulch again?’ Everett asked. ‘You could keep your head low like before.’

The Kid stood and walked to the open door. He inhaled deeply as the older man moved to his side.

‘I tried that, Clem.’

The lawman rubbed his neck.

‘What you mean?’

Valko turned his head and looked into the weathered face. ‘When I rode back to Dry Gulch, Sheriff Tom Clyde was waiting for me on the trail. He said that a bunch of bounty hunters had arrived a few days ago and were holed up around my ranch. They were waiting to get the drop on me.’

Everett’s eyes narrowed and he gritted his teeth angrily.

‘Someone must have trailed me before when I went to ask you if you’d help me. It must have something to do with those evil varmints in Austin.’

‘Twenty-five thousand bucks is a lot of temptation, Clem.’ Valko smiled.

'I'm sorry, Kid.'

Valko shrugged. He picked his reins off the hitching rail and gathered them up in his hands. His eyes darted all around the busy street as he stepped off the boardwalk and into his stirrup.

'I can't ever go back there, Clem.'

Everett suddenly felt sober.

'Where are you headed, Valko?'

The young man ran a hand along his stallion's neck.

'Wherever Snow wants to go, I reckon.'

'You want company?' asked the lawman, stepping to the edge of the boardwalk.

The Kid looked down into the man's sad eyes. There was a desperation in them that matched his own.

'It's a long, lonely trail.'

'I've nothing left here for me, Kid,' Everett admitted. 'Only memories. Most of which are darn painful.'

The Valko Kid turned his mount and stared along the crowded street. He did not look at Everett as he spoke.

'Reckon old Snow here could use the company of that skinny horse you call Blue, if his master's willing to ride with a living target.'

Clem Everett nodded. 'I figure Blue's master's willing, Kid.'

The Valko Kid turned his horse again and began to ride away from the office.

'Where you going?' Everett called out.

Valko eased back on his reins and the magnificent stallion paused as the Kid looked over his broad shoulder.

'We're going to the livery stable, Clem. That is where you keep that long-legged gelding, ain't it? You coming?'

Clem Everett unpinned his marshal's star and tossed it on to the desk. He grabbed his hat and ran down the centre of the street. Valko reached down and grabbed his friend's arm. He scooped Everett off his feet. The marshal landed on the saddle cantle behind the smiling young outlaw.

'Let's ride, son.'

'Are you sure, Clem?'

'Yep!'

The Valko Kid tapped his boots against his mount's sides and steered Snow towards the livery stables. When he reached the wooden building he reined in and watched as the marshal dropped to the ground and ran through the open doors.

Within five minutes Blue was saddled.

The two riders rode out of the bustling Waco and into the darkness. If either had a future awaiting him, he knew that they would face it together.

We do hope that you have enjoyed reading this large print book.

Did you know that all of our titles are available for purchase?

We publish a wide range of high quality large print books including:
Romances, Mysteries, Classics
General Fiction
Non Fiction and Westerns

Special interest titles available in large print are:
The Little Oxford Dictionary
Music Book, Song Book
Hymn Book, Service Book

Also available from us courtesy of Oxford University Press:
Young Readers' Dictionary
(large print edition)
Young Readers' Thesaurus
(large print edition)

For further information or a free brochure, please contact us at:

Other titles in the
Linford Western Library:

THE HIDDEN APACHES

Mike Stall

Phil Roche, the foremost gambler on the Mississippi riverboats, was an exacting man. To cheat him and live, you had to be quicker on the draw. So far nobody had been. But all that changed when he heard that Susan had been murdered and her child, Lucie, kidnapped. The Apaches seemed to be the prime suspects. Now the people of Lanchester County would discover that Roche could be just as tough outside the casino. But his search for Lucie uncovers more than he had bargained for . . .